The Plum Rains & Other Stories

Other Titles by John Givens

Sons of the Pioneers
(Harcourt Brace Jovanovich, New York)

A Friend in the Police
(Harcourt Brace Jovanovich, New York)

Living Alone
(Atheneum, New York)

A Guide to Dublin Bay
(The Liffey Press, Dublin)

Irish Walled Towns
(The Liffey Press, Dublin)

The Plum Rains

& Other Stories

John Givens

The Liffey Press

Published by
The Liffey Press,
Ashbrook House, 10 Main Street
Raheny, Dublin 5, Ireland
www.theliffeypress.com

A catalogue record of this book is
available from the British Library.

ISBN 978-1-905785-76-6

Some of these stories originally appeared in the following
publications, often in very different versions: 'The Green
Summer Wind' in *Kyoto Journal*, 'The Buddha-nature of the
Horse' in *The Mississippi Review Online*, 'Bushclover and the
Moon' in *Cerise Press*, 'The Pariah Supervisor' in *Night Train*,' The
Emptiness Monk in *Eclectica*, 'The Plantain' in *Necessary Fiction*,
'Abnegation' in *Ashé Journal*, 'Lightness' in *Cerise Press*, and 'The
Plum Rains' in *Wag's Revue*. The author is grateful to the editors
of these journals for permission to reprint.

Printed and bound in the UK by the MPG Books Group,
Bodmin and King's Lynn

Contents

Author's Note

After centuries of feudal warfare, the Tokugawa family unified Japan in 1601 and established a new capital in Edo, the city that would eventually become Tokyo. The Tokugawa were samurai, members of the hereditary warrior class whose behaviour was defined by the mediaeval code of *bushidō*. Loyalty, frugality, mastery of martial arts, and personal honour were essential principles for the samurai, as was the requirement to die a good death. Peace meant their fighting skills were no longer required, however, and as samurai were not permitted to work at any other kind of occupation, many became destitute.

The decline of the samurai was matched by the rise of the merchant; the city replaced the castle as the centre of culture and commerce; and medieval aesthetics yielded to popular new urban forms, such as the kabuki theatre, *haikai* linked poetry — precursor to haiku — and even the novel. Some samurai became bureaucrats or farmers, and some became professional artists and poets, most notably among them Matsuo Bashō (1644–1694), a man who is widely regarded today as Japan's greatest writer. But there were also samurai who could not accept the new world that was arriving, and they became hired swords or even brigands. Japan's modern yakuza gangsters often like to see themselves as descendants of rogue samurai.

These stories are set in the last decade of the seventeenth century. Bashō is at the centre of several of them. Others describe characters who are unwilling or unable to find a place for themselves. There are impoverished samurai struggling against their own uselessness, young female pleasure providers who wish to be more than playthings for rich merchants, a range of other early-modern Japanese types, from gamblers to senior shogunate officials, and an outcast who rises through his own merit.

I've long been interested in Japanese literary forms, and I've fused the requirements of the seventeenth century with contemporary prose expectations. Some of these stories function as martial tales, and some as modernised versions of Buddhist debate dialogues. The travel narrative is particularly Japanese, and many of these stories portray figures in motion through a landscape. A form unique to Japan is the *haibun*, a prose version of *haikai* poetry which evolved out of head notes setting the scene for poems and often seems both discursive and compressed. But ultimately, my aim with these stories is to present a world that while very different from our own, still resonates with the pleasure of what it means to be human.

John Givens
Howth, Co Dublin
January 2010

The Green Summer Wind

夏の青風

An old man sat gazing out on summer mountains stacked beneath a white sky, the heated masses of green and blue-green resolving themselves back into the more distant layers of brown and beige and dove grey before leaching away finally into a pale wash of heat haze.

Bashō removed his round travel hat and dried his face and head with a clean white cloth then picked up his hat again and fanned himself with it. His road companion, Chibi-kun, sprawled beside him and drew circles in the dirt. They were dressed alike in the lightweight summer robes of wandering monks. Each wore a woven hemp travel satchel and sleeping quilt tied diagonally across one shoulder, and each had a water gourd suspended from his obi sash. Their hands and forearms were darkened from the summer sun, and summer road dust coated their feet and ankles.

You must be getting tired, the old man said; and Chibi-kun – a youth postponing the burdens of adult responsibility – looked away and said nothing, the better to enjoy feeling sorry for himself.

They had shaved their heads on the day of their departure, then shaved them again after twenty days on the walking road, and the stubble now was of a length that made the old man long for the bite of a fat-blade razor. He had equipped himself with a hardwood staff, and Chibi-kun was outfitted with a woven bamboo carryall for the utensils they required. The boy also had various prophylactic amulets tucked away here and there on his person as a defence against goblins and water sprites. Although his birth-status allowed him to wear the two swords of a samurai, Old Master Bashō would permit neither of them to carry a weapon, much to his companion's disgust.

Shall we continue?

I'm too tired.

You want to stay here?

Here? The boy looked around and assessed their surroundings or pretended to. This wretched place?

Bashō drank from his water gourd then replaced the stopper, screwing it down into the gourd-mouth tightly. He tied on his sun hat and readjusted his equipment then hitched up the hem of his summer robe, secured the front flap of it under his obi sash in the manner of the old-style foot-pilgrims and set off again.

The boy ignored his departure. He studied his dirty pink toes. But when the old man rounded a bend and didn't look back, Chibi-kun jumped up and scurried after him. Wait, can't you! he cried. Such discourtesy!

The path they followed led up into a dense cedar forest. It was wide enough for walking men to pass each other without loss of dignity, or even for men on horseback to manage it; but if two palanquins met, one would have to yield to the other, and even in this era of the Shogun's Great Peace, such encounters were fraught.

We should have gone another way, said Chibi-kun petulantly.

There was no other way.

Then we should have found one!

Chibi-kun was a child of new times. Clever with words, a precocious literary prodigy, he was the youngest of the Old Master's linked poetry disciples and much favoured by him. During formal group sessions, the fertility of his imagination would send the boy flying past his more cautious elders; and he would burst out with suggestions even when it wasn't his turn. Creating solitary sequences was more satisfying for the boy. And what delighted him most was the rapid-fire composition of a single-poet sequence before an audience of admirers. Modern *haikai* linked poems were composed of thirty-six stanzas, each building off the one before; but Chibi-kun so trusted his own vitality that he would take on the traditional hundred-stanza sequence and even the occasional thousand-stanza effort, audaciously tossing off link after link in a fever of creativity so that even two scribes with quick brushes would have to scramble to keep up with him.

The boy never rewrote. What audience ever cared to sit through the process of a revision? Your first idea was your best idea, and these tedious old plodders struggling to choose between 'winter drizzle' and 'wintry gusts' left him gasping with impatience. Chibi-kun loved the bustle of the new cities of Edo and Osaka and Sakai, with their theatres and teahouses and the salons of rich merchants; but what suited him best were the lush pleasure gardens of powerful daimyo warlords, where his charm and inventiveness could be savoured at leisure by himself and others. These wild northern mountains were disagreeable to the boy – nothing at all like the screen paintings of them that he admired – and he stumbled along, thinking only of what he would say at his next opportunity to extend the range of his disappointments.

The two walkers continued up through the shadowy forest, their footsteps muffled by a thick duff of dry cedar sprays so that the old path resembled the course of a hillside stream made rufous with silt; and even the incessant screech of cicadas seemed muted here by the wet heat of the day and weight of the closely-spaced cedars.

They rounded a bend to discover a landslip spill of raw boulders blocking their path, like a tumble of petrified dragon scat rolled down out of the mountainside and leaving a ragged gash in the red soil. Look at this! Chibi-kun cried. What a nuisance! The drop-off was steep and they were obliged to negotiate the obstruction with care, loose scree giving way and rattling like hailstones into the gorge far below. Who's responsible for maintaining this road?

Mountain bogeys, said the Old Master. Hopping goblins with long red noses.

No doubt hoping for a poem from you, the boy muttered, intentionally climbing over a large boulder instead of taking the easier way around it.

Ogres and bogeys were real to the boy because of his own heightened sense of self-worth. For Chibi-kun, every event, every happenstance – no matter how remote – could still be connected to him by the jewel-cord of a karmic irrevocability so that if a sea-fiend were known to have victimised some unfortunate wretch on a fishing boat far offshore, it was nevertheless still somehow Chibi-kun himself who must have been the weird malignancy's ultimate concern, and the shudder of compassion the boy felt was always personal.

The cedar forest thinned as the walkers climbed, and the ferns and clumps of wild orchids that thrived in filtered light gave way to sturdy patches of dwarf bamboo grass and gaps choked with mahonia, the masses of prickly branches hung with shiny purple-black berries that glistened like death's own seeds in the windy sunlight.

You can't eat those, Bashō cautioned, always willing to be helpful when help wasn't needed; and Chibi-kun made no response, hoping the old fellow might worry that he'd done so already.

They climbed up into an area of exposed rock that extended under the summer sky like a gods' platform, the grey expanse of it sun-flattened, wind-hammered, encrusted with lichens and gripped by a few stunted pines with thick roots fitted down into crevice fractures for the life to be found there; and they rounded a sweeping curve with their robe-sleeves flapping then emerged onto a broad shelf of naked granite that was thrust out over the void like an immense stone fist striking the empty air.

What! We have to stop *again*?

Old Master Bashō found a smooth spot and sank down facing the opposite slopes. The shimmering fabric of cedars and cypresses was splashed here and there with brighter patches of maples and camphor trees, and the whole of it rose up in a steep green verticality that undulated beneath the combing fingers of the wind like the flapping of an immense sail.

The boy flopped down beside him. These mountains all look the same.

Bashō opened his travel pouch and removed his writing kit, a bronze brush-holder ending in a bulbous pot stuffed with ink-soaked cotton fibers and fabricated to look like a leek fused onto a ball onion.

He sucked briefly on the dried tip of his brush to soften it, leaving a black smudge on his lips, then unrolled his travel journal until he found where he had left off. He stared out at the wind-flow on the flanks of the mountains, with the heat of the sun on the granite and the tumbling rush of a stream in the gorge below; then he brush-wrote a couplet of parallel five-character lines in Chinese:

Green upon green, the summer mountain wind;
Farther and farther, the plantain at my hut.

He studied what he had made then looked up. The wind gusted stronger as he watched, and the summer forests tossed and trembled as if the mountains were reaching out to each other.

Can we go yet?

I thought you were tired.

Of course I'm tired!

Then you should rest more.

A furious racket erupted below them, and a troop of apes burst out of the stream-side bamboo, tumbling and screeching and baring their fangs, launching reprisals in all directions although nothing beyond their own tumult seemed to be threatening them. Too volatile to settle on any strategy, advantages gained by one were soon lost to another, and the apes finally scattered out of sight, spun away by the centrifugal force of their own agitation.

Old Master Bashō returned to his writing. He composed a phrase in their own language, the words connected each to the next in a single, sinuous line of ink that swept down with casual ease:

A summer gale in the mountains, and the wild monkeys also struggle to find shelter.

Next to this he wrote:

A summer downpour in the mountains, and the wild monkeys also seem to want little rain capes.

He studied this line for a moment then blotted out *A summer downpour in the mountains*, hatching across each character with strokes like bird-tracks in snow.

Now can we go?

Bashō gazed out at the flowing mountains before him then brush-wrote *The first drizzle* beside the opening phrase he'd effaced, sat pondering what he'd done then added *A winter shower* next to that line then next to it *Freezing sleet.*

Why are you doing all that?

7

I'll need ideas.

Those are winter images. You can't use them for an opening stanza made in summer.

I know. But even in summer, mountains feel like a place of winter to me.

To me, they're just an inconvenience.

The Old Master pondered the phrases he had made then scraped the ink residue off his brush by drawing it backwards along the surface of a rock to maintain the integrity of the tip. He was known everywhere as a poet who looked at everything he saw, and who cherished the words he used to describe the occurrences of the world yet also distrusted this fondness so that the phrases he devised often left him dissatisfied. There was no remedy for it. He would assemble variations even as he recognised the folly of his desire to determine somehow the one perfect way of saying what in his heart he knew could never be said.

You get past one mountain and there's another one, Chibi-kun declared. Like it was waiting for you.

What the Old Master wanted was to make statements of his own that could be placed beside those made by men of the past and deserve to be there with them. His journeys were pilgrimages, but his religion was the way of *haikai* linked poetry. He wandered through remote provinces in order to perfect his manner by testing himself against the austerities of travel, going where his precursors had gone and seeing the world as they'd seen it. But his celebrity preceded him wherever he went, and access to men of the past became buried beneath the importuning of those living in the present. Nothing could be done. Rustic magnates would insist on entertaining him for as long as he could be persuaded to stay. They would invite fellow aesthetes; and after a sequence had been completed and each participant written out his own fair copy for the glory of his name and the edification of his heirs, they would fill the afternoons and evenings with feasting and singing so that the holy silence of the mountains rang loudly with their praise of it.

The Old Master slid his writing brush into the tube holder and fitted the cap back onto the ball-onion ink pot.

You can't start a linked poem made in summer with a winter image! Chibi-kun cried, casting about for a way to connect one disappointment to another. And you'll be asked to lead some stupid group in the next castle-town. Causing us more delays. He scowled at his own dust-covered feet. More waiting, more tedium. He thought about it. More dirty old fingers pulling on me.

The path climbed higher and curved back under the expanse of an up-flung face of granite. The two walkers passed through the cool blue shadows of the cliff-side without pausing and re-emerged into the afternoon sunlight. A hawk tilted high above them, adjusting itself with the delicacy of an unconsidered skill; and at the next bend they came upon a mountain quince, stunted and gnarled, and with a spattering of late-season blossoms still glowing on it like dusty little discs of fire. A child's skeleton lay beneath the lower boughs of the old tree, the collection of small bones draped in places with scraps of rotting cloth like objects meant for such display. The Old Master drew closer. His shadow fell across the child's skeleton, and he quickly moved to one side to avoid the desecration.

Why's that like that? Chibi-kun demanded.

I don't know. Tufts of summer grass sprouted up among the curved ivory bows of the child's rib box. Probably he died here.

I told you this wasn't a good way!

The little skull's jawbone was missing; and the bowl of the skull had twisted off to one side, as if when sliding down onto his death-glide the child had wished to look at something other than what he had been seeing.

Old Master Bashō knelt beside the bone scatter. He removed his round sedge-grass travel hat and bent forward to observe what proved to be a handful of mouse pups nestled within the cup of the brain case, pink and hairless little newborns, their tiny toes perfect, tiny tails like curved pink filaments, lovely little breathers without blemish bedded on shreds of the dead child's garments that had been dragged inside by mouse parents intent on the comfort of their progeny.

There's something written there, Chibi-kun said, unwilling to touch what he'd found.

Words had been inked onto a piece of cotton fabric that was attached with a hemp cord to the dead child's tarsus.

The Old Master was concerned with the explanations men devised to soothe themselves because he himself needed soothing; and he read out the declaration that had been dictated by starving parents to some local priest or other mountain literate, asserting that this child entrusted here to his fate was a good child, obedient and loved, and that he had been relegated to this desolation through no fault of his own but simply because he was the weakest member of a despairing family that had been crushed by the civil wars and retained no hope for succour or salvation. Whosoever wanted him was hereby authorised to adopt him as their own. The child would answer to the name 'Saburō' although another name could be attached if his finder so preferred.

Do you think they really believed someone would take the child?

Perhaps they tried to believe it.

Could they have just walked away? Chibi-kun was outraged by it. With the child's sobs in their ears? Could a mother do that? Turn her back? With the little child holding out his little arms and pleading to be picked up and carried with them?

The Old Master remained as he was. I don't know.

A wretched place to die, Chibi-kun said, letting his anger become disgust and his disgust become scorn. These wretched people, these stupid ugly victims that die so easily...

But the Old Master only reached out and took the red-orange blossoms of the child's quince in his hand, holding it for a long moment and gazing down at the beauty of the fiery orange discs blazing there in the windy sunlight with all the fragility and tenacity of being, and he held it and held it then let it go.

The Buddha-nature of the Horse
馬の仏性

Head throbbing, throat parched, his mouth tasting like he'd been sucking on his feet, the rogue samurai Hasegawa Torakage came awake and felt for his small sword. It was there beside him, black iron hilt guard without ornamentation, a money-fighter's choice.

So he had that much.

But he also had the summer stench of indigo boiling.

And under his light quilt, he was naked, not even wearing a loincloth.

Hasegawa's other hand drifted behind him surreptitiously, seeking any companion who might still be with him, some pinch-faced little squirmer from the night before to whom promises had been imprudently made. Detecting only the wooden surface of floor planking, he lifted himself up on one elbow and peered out at this man-deceiving world of error and delusion through pain-stricken, red-rimmed eyes. Koda? he called.

There was no display alcove in the shabby little room where he'd spent the night, no floor mats, no brazier, not even a tobacco box; and the wall plaster had fallen away in places to reveal a support-lattice of bamboo strips like flattened yellow bones. A *hokku* head-stanza by Old Master Bashō had been painted on one wall in an exuberant if shaky hand:

Morning dew on the damp earth, and the muddy melons seem cool.

The borrowed inkstone and calligraphy brush he must have used to write it were left lying nearby.

Koda? he called again and was again met with silence.

Hasegawa lay back to settle the pounding in his head. Occasionally, when harassed or anticipating harassment, he would string what cash money he possessed onto a spare sandal cord and bind it to one ankle. Although he had no recollection of having done anything preparatory, there was always the possibility of it. A cursory reconnaissance confirmed that his nakedness was complete, and he sat up, bracing himself against the serpents-nest of nausea that rose up uncoiling within him. Ko-*da*! It sounded like the cry of a gut-stuck boar.

The wine had seemed cloudy and unclean in the wineshop last night, and he recalled confiding as much to his cousin but then forgetting this sensible evaluation as the evening progressed, the day's exhaustion receded, and the good-fellowship shared among travellers on the walking road led him from folly to folly.

Koda would have said nothing. He himself drank only water and ate very little, as if his diminutive body's refusal to grow relieved him of any responsibility for coddling it. Koda practised mountain-monk austerities and could go for days without eating or sleeping then charge into a squad of opponents and scatter them like pond frogs. Koda indulged his younger cousin's habits of conviviality, and Hasegawa's high spirits and easy generosity brought the world to their table; but even the most dimwitted of roisterers could not settle fully into an evening of mirth and mayhem until the dour – and dangerous – older man had left the wineshop.

Hasegawa crawled to the entryway and slid open the paper door, wincing against the shock of summer sunlight. His stomach lifted again and rolled upward in a column of snake-bile that burned at the bottom of his throat until he forced it back down. Never would he drink cloudy wine again. Ever. His room opened onto a dirt garden that was dominated by an immense camphor tree, the mass of it richly green. Near the tree stood a privy; and the rogue samurai vomited into the loathsome hole, emptying himself in great splattering waves of pain that burned up the length of him as they came. Maggots wriggled in the foulness below him like bits of chewed noodle come back to life, and Hasegawa retched again and again until he was producing little more than a dry spittle. He straightened up too abruptly, lurched to one side, overcorrected, and crashed backwards through the privy door, knocking it off its runners as he emerged wobble-walking into the garden and fetching up finally at the trunk of the camphor tree where he clung like a baby ape clutching its mother.

Hasegawa saw now that his clothing had been strung along a bamboo laundry-drying pole suspended under the eaves of the building where he'd spent the night, and his other possessions were there in a neat pile beneath it. He retrieved his clothing and sorted through his travel satchel. Only a few copper coins remained at the end of what should have been a nearly full string; yet his writing kit was still there, as was a hiding dagger, a *Jizō-bosatsu* in a little metal reliquary, and other objects of value that any easy-way boy would have carried off.

A young maid approached from an indigo dyer's shop next door, the long strips of freshly dyed cotton cloth suspended from tall poles like war banners against the milky white sky. She carried a pot of tea and a cup and an earthenware jar of water cold from the well. Also on her tray was a covered bowl with two rice cakes wrapped in laver. The dyer's maid bowed timidly and deposited her tray on the veranda corridor with an awkward clatter.

Where's Koda? Hasegawa demanded, and the young woman lowered her eyes. Who is Koda? Her teeth had not been blackened properly, and the flashes of whiteness surprised him. Your honour's road companion?

He was with me.

You mean here at the waystation?

Where else would I mean? Hasegawa poured out his tea himself. Did we meet last night?

She glanced up at him shyly. Meet?

Do you not understand the language I speak?

Do you not remember last night?

Hasegawa looked at her. Some parts of it better than others.

The maid lowered her eyes again, as if abashed at her boldness.

Hasegawa studied the immense camphor tree, the bright shining mass of yellow-green leaves glowing in the fullness of summer. Yesterday my cousin and I walked without stopping all the way from the seventeenth waystation. A distance that usually requires two full days.

The maid bowed to indicate her recognition of the wondrous nature of this achievement. Your honour has important affairs awaiting you in the Old Imperial City.

I meant only to express the source of my confusion. We arrived well after dusk. And thoroughly exhausted.

Yes, of course, the young maid agreed. Yet you seemed very lively last night.

Giddiness caused by excessive exhaustion.

The maid smiled. Clearly that must be the fact of it. But do you not remember singing the libretto of the Noh play? About the old woman damned to suffer as a wandering ghost because she had been unfeeling when young and beautiful?

Of course I remember that. A scattering of sparrows had begun dropping down into the courtyard in twos and threes, squabbling little brown feather-balls riotous with their enthusiasms. Now that you mention it.

All in the wineshop were favourably impressed.

Hasegawa said nothing.

And do you not then remember buying the carcass of the dead cart horse so that it might receive a decent funeral?

A grey horse, as I recall…

You said it would thereby find release from the sadness of birth after birth. And that it would thus reach the Western Paradise. And share a golden lotus throne with the Amida Buddha. And now her eyes were twinkling with amusement. A horse, you see.

Hasegawa again studied the camphor tree against the soft morning haze of the summer sky. A few sparrows moved among the exposed roots searching for insects while others settled into patches of loose dirt and began taking dust baths, wing-flurries creating furious little beige clouds.

All in the wineshop praised your sensitivity. And your sense of pity for the Buddha-soul of the unfortunate horse.

I paid for it, did I?

The young woman smiled. Very generously.

He sipped his tea. I guess that's all right then.

Hasegawa Torakage had found himself among the hacked ruins of men he hadn't known were enemies. He had watched their blood-flow draining away into summer grasses or pooling on the frozen earth of a winter's night, the dead and dying men like him, men whose companionship he might otherwise have shared; and he had trusted what was happening to them and not sought to follow back out along the chain of irrevocable consequences and determine the one true source of their undoing. Hasegawa was a fighter who accepted the inevitability of the fact of convergence. Their deaths had wanted them as would one day his want him. So he sat with the pungent scent of indigo burdening the lush summer air, the chirr of cicadas shrill enough to pierce any stone, and the uncertainty of the young maid who bowed, waited to see if he had further require-

ments of her, then bowed again and departed, leaving
him to his ruminations and his tea.

KODA WAS SQUATTING just inside the gate-shadows of a
roadside shrine, his too-long sword held upright between his knees, the oversized grip of it rising high
above his small dark head like a finial of defiance. I
guess I know what you're going to say, Hasegawa said.
So probably you don't have to say it.

Koda Ichinosuke wore his topknot crazy-style, the
fore-crown unshaven and the tea-whisk of hair sticking
straight up in a cockscomb of comic bravado. His robe
was a concatenation of mismatched fabrics sewn together in frantic unsuitability: a pomegranate red patch
beside a cobalt blue one, a venomous green panel next
to one with purplish-brown stripes on a beige field, a
long pale-azure section printed all over with scarlet spider lilies fitted beside an orange field splashed with indigo sea shells and bordering a taupe strip gaudy with
sprays of kerria blossoms that had been dyed to a bil-
ious yellow. It was a harlequin provocation, unmistak-
able in its intention; and any scabbard-brusher who encountered Koda had to know that here was his own
death approaching. All he need do was remark upon
the small man's bizarre appearance or smile wrong at
the sight of him, or even just smile at all.

What Koda loved was the prick of the point of an
arrowhead tested against the ball of the thumb, the pull
of the rattan-wrapped bamboo bow and the music of its
string-release, the flight of the arrow and the irrevocability of its impact. He cherished the shock of a spear

thrust through a paper door, and the cunning use of a fat-blade halberd as a limb-lopper. He had also developed an expertise in the original method of tight-space indoor fighting with a small sword or even a slash knife filleting in close. For Koda, the form it took was irrelevant. What he trusted was his ability to find within any given moment the optimal route to the next.

Koda's main sword was twice as long as it should have been. The scabbard for this field-harvester was lacquered bright scarlet; and written in a bold calligraphy down its flank was the motto *An Ugly Runt Deserves Chastisement,* the thick black characters meant to be legible at a distance. Although a poor choice for a small man, in his hands the too-long sword carved great sibilant arcs out of the air, its passage like sheet lightning noticed an instant too late. But for all his pleasure in it, Koda would also offer to trade weapons or use another, lesser blade or even one of his opponent's own choosing so as to demonstrate that the accomplishment belonged to the hands of the holder and not the thing held. Koda was willing to fight with wooden cudgels if he met someone so inclined, or with iron hand-clubs or sharpened bamboo poles or pointed cedar stakes; he would batter with rocks if that was required, or cut with shards of clam shell or bits of chipped flint; he would kick and punch with the feet and the fists, strike with elbows and knees, and butt with the head; he would bite and gouge, strangle and smother, drown opponents in cisterns, lakes, streams, ponds and canals, hang them from ropes, fling them off cliffs, or stuff them into fires. It never occur to you how maybe someday you might want to try making friends with somebody? his cousin had once asked him; and Koda had thought he meant as a deceptive tactic. You start thinking that way, you've probably already lost.

I guess probably you could say how you were right about that wine, Hasegawa said.

His cousin stood slowly, his small brown face bland as that of a basking viper.

I guess it was a good lesson for me. That what you think?

Koda returned Hasegawa's scrutiny for a moment then turned away and began walking back into the centre of the waystation village, his too-long sword resting comfortably across one shoulder much the way a peasant might tote a mattock.

Hasegawa Torakage had been orphaned as a child of six and gone to live with the Koda family in the far north. His cousin Ichinosuke was five years older, and when the boys trained with wooden practice swords, Ichinosuke always won. Even after Torakage had grown larger and stronger than his cousin, their mock battles always ended with him lying on the ground. He tried changing tactics. He tried hanging back and countering with short-stroke defensive parries. He tried deception, circling the wrong way and hitting out of odd angles. He tried quick-flicker cuts at his cousin's hands and forearms, at his knees and ankles, all of which seemed exposed but never were. He tried to distract his cousin with mockery and flattery and mindless jibber-jabber, and he tried to seal within himself a perfected clarity of irresistible depth and audacity before beginning his attack. The results were always the same. He tried a reasoned and well-grounded approach to the problem, and he tried overwhelming power, battering at the smaller boy in an hysterical frenzy. Each encounter ended with Hasegawa Torakage sprawled on the ground, stunned and bleeding, and his cousin standing over him, curious to see if he would try again.

The drayman was waiting in front of the waystation corral. He had lived all his life with horses and over the years had grown to resemble them. No woman would share his habits so the drayman had never married. Whores demanded double-fees because of the pungency of his musk, and wineshops discouraged his patronage for the same reason.

The drayman had spotted the two rogue samurai approaching, and he elected to display voluntarily the coins clutched in his fist rather than risk being made to do so.

This seems to be the full amount of it, Hasegawa said. Minus two coppers.

Koda looked at him.

I guess that must be the real price for the funeral rites for a horse here.

Koda began walking back through the waystation village. One copper for the Buddha-soul of the horse, he said. Also, the drayman took care of your money for you last night. One copper for that.

A boy had been left tethered to a tree at the edge of the waystation horse meadow. He was a stunted little shirker, wearing a stained and grimy short-robe held closed by a sash woven out of crudely dyed fibers. His hair wasn't trimmed, he chewed off his fingernails like a creature gone feral, and a fuzz of hairs darkened his upper lip and chin. The boy had the comfort of the tree's shade, and his rope let him move to the edge of a stream but no farther.

Koda kept going but Hasegawa stopped. He asked him why he was being restrained, and the boy said because he stole food.

Why did he do that?

When his father was absent, his stepmother denied him his share. And even when his father was home, she gave his stepsister the best bits while he got only the worst.

Where was his father?

The boy didn't know.

Why didn't his father defend him?

The boy didn't know that either.

Hasegawa handed him a rice ball and the feral boy bit into it. Do you want me to cut you out of your ropes?

The boy said he didn't want that.

Because it would anger your stepmother? Hasegawa squatted down beside him. At least you've got tree shade. And water.

You're samurai.

That's right.

You know about things.

Some things.

The feral boy said he'd been told that a stabbing tool could be fashioned out of a sharpened length of green bamboo. He said he understood that anyone could do

22

it. You just had to get the angle of the bevel right. He said there was said to be a place in a sleeping woman's neck where her death was easily reached.

Hasegawa looked up at his cousin then turned his attention back to the meadow grass heating in the sunlight, swallows darting above it taking insects, a patch of scarlet spider lilies near the road embankment, all of it wrapped within the endless cacophony of cicadas shrieking their summer urges. And you don't know where it is.

They said you just slide it in.

Who says that?

I forget his name.

And you think you could kill a person?

The boy chewed, bits of cold rice on his lips, his gaze unwavering. I guess that's what we're talking about.

How old are you?

Old enough.

You think so.

The boy pointed at his own neck. Just show me where it is.

Hasegawa rose to his feet and stood pondering the feral boy gnawing at the rice ball in his grubby fist. Did he have any other siblings?

Just the one. The stepmother's own daughter.

And you want to hurt her too.

Hurt them both. But start with the stepmother. Just ease it in.

You don't need to know about things like that.

You mean you won't say. The boy grinned up at

him, his face serenely vicious. You're some poor kind of samurai, aren't you. I guess you just chop cabbages with those blades.

Cut him loose, Koda said.

He said he didn't want that.

But Koda was on the boy with a slash knife in his fist, and the rope came apart, the severed ends lying on each side of him. You want to be tied up, you do it yourself.

The two samurai continued out onto the dust of the Eastern Sea Road, the sun pounding down and the cicadas shrieking their summer urges.

I guess probably you don't think that a horse has a Buddha-nature, Hasegawa said.

Koda said nothing.

I guess you could look at it two ways. One way, that everything has a Buddha-nature. A horse, a tree, a rock, a man. Everything. And the other way, that only a man can have the Buddha-nature and everything else has something different. Of course, I guess whichever way you choose, you'd still have the question of how you would know. But then I guess you'd always have that question anyway. How you know, I mean.

So I guess one thing you could do is you could debate it. I could for example assert that a horse has the Buddha-nature. You could take the opposing view. So then I would state the reasons why I held my belief, and you would question them and perhaps point out certain aspects of the matter which I hadn't considered. So your suggestions would then require me to rethink my original decision and perhaps adjust some portion of it. Which I would do. Then you would perhaps state your beliefs, and I would bring out my arguments in light of your understanding of things. And then you could reply as you saw fit. And so in this manner, we could spend the day in pleasant conversation. Except of course we can't. Since you never say much of anything one way or the other. So I guess there's no reason for me to go on about it.

Then don't, Koda said.

Bushclover and the Moon

萩 と 月

A true son of Edo, high-spirited, candid, and fond of all things new and novel, the Lesser Tada doted on imported teas, polychrome crockery, lacquered trays inlaid with mother-of-pearl, sweet bean-paste cakes, salacious drawings, fragrant hair oils, and cunningly wrought ivory baubles attached as toggles on sash-pouches, his favourite being a rare hinged specimen depicting two baboons squat-fucking, the realistic action of which was much admired by connoisseurs, who found in the precision of its mechanism and the audacity of its design a demonstration of the superiority of the culture of the Edo townsman.

The Lesser Tada's unlined summer robe of indigo cotton was modest enough, but sewn around the insides of the neckband and sleeve openings were strips of lavender silk that he was in the habit of stroking with his fingertips. His oiled coif was stylishly arranged and held in place with a twisted paper cord the pale milky blue of the summer sky, and he wore his bright scarlet loincloth with the front flap hanging down, an urban affectation thought shocking in rural districts.

No doubt my smaller girl has read all your linked poems, the Lesser Tada declared to the celebrated *haikai* poet with whom he had offered to share his accommodations at the inn. Or at least the most famous ones. The man himself was no reader.

The soaking tub in the back garden was an elongated trough formed from thick cedar planks and fed through a bamboo trickle-pipe furred rufous with iron. Rinsing buckets were piled nearby, and the two bathers perched on low stools in the hazy summer sunlight and began scrubbing themselves with their hand towels, the assignations man entertaining Old Master Bashō with offers and opinions and gossip.

The Tada brothers were well-established in Edo's pleasure quarters of Yoshiwara. The elder brother's teahouse catered to an exclusive clientele of wealthy pleasure-seekers while the Lesser Tada's own public rooms were open to any person with sufficient funds for the food and drink and saucy banter provided there. You have to know how to read your customers, explained the Lesser Tada, wringing out his hand towel, and be open to fresh ideas. No person not totally impoverished was too poor for the House of the Lesser Tada, and even the possessor of but a single copper coin gripped in a care-worn fist would be included in an evening's merriment for the time required to strip it from him.

Shall we call for some rice wine? A plate of titbits perhaps?

Perhaps later, Bashō said.

The Lesser Tada thought his brother was old-fashioned. The man produced pleasure banquets attended by grand courtesans who sat simpering within immense mounds of silk brocade, their heads immobilised by the need to manage massive chignons freighted with an arsenal of tortoise-shell combs and thrust pins and silver hair ornaments. Grand courtesans epitomised the brilliance of the traditions of the floating world of desire. But their heightened sense of self-magnificence made them difficult to approach so that much cajoling and entreaty was required to accomplish even the most superficial of transmissions. And this, friend, if I may say it, said the Lesser Tada, after all financial expectations have been satisfied. He rinsed off then scuttled across to the big cedar-wood soaking trough and climbed in, damson-sack dangling. There's a better way of providing for the needs of the shogun's city, said the Lesser Tada, pleased with himself and his candour, a more modern way; and sighing with contentment, he sank deeply into the pungent heat of the murky water.

The Lesser Tada's assignations teahouse had been among the first to promote young serving maids as peony girls, selecting those with a lively manner and sweet disposition, outfitting them in gaudy robes then encouraging them to feel emotions and share their feelings widely.

What does Edo have in abundance? The Lesser Tada answered his own question: Samurai bumpkins with time to fill and money to spend. And what else? The sons of rich merchants with even more money available. And what do they want? Their food served and their wine poured? Someone dancing, someone singing, someone banging away on the three-string? Is that all? Smutty chitchat? Finger games? And then of course as occurs in the natural order of things – he hurried past it in deference to the famous poet's no doubt heightened sensibility – access to the release of the carnal inclination. But can that be all? The Lesser Tada draped his hand towel on top of his head. More than that, friend, if I can say it, he said, and leaned in towards Old Master Bashō confidingly. A chance for love. An opportunity for the joys and heartbreaks of romantic love.

The grand courtesans cannot provide it?

Hardly. Grand courtesans are like the decorated tower-floats of the Gion festival that are dragged through the streets of the Old Imperial Capital at the start of summer, beautiful to look at but massive and ponderous and –

And what would *you* know about it? called Oyuki, the larger and bolder of his peony girls as she advanced across the back garden, her hand towel held draped down over her loins with casual and sluttish aplomb. Have *you* ever pulled on one?

Oyuki and Ohasu had bound up their elaborate coiffures with white head-cloths to preserve the shapes of them. They kicked off their garden clogs and squatted near the dipping buckets then began scrubbing themselves vigourously, rubbing their skin pink.

You can buy wine anywhere in the pleasure quarters, the Lesser Tada continued, tasty food, lively music, a quilt-companion, female or male. But can dreams reach no higher? Is that all there is be wished for? I think we can agree it is not. Hearts aflame, that's what's wanted! Burning with love's ardour!

Stomachs burning from cheap wine, muttered bold Oyuki; and little Ohasu laughed then glanced shyly at the famous *haikai* poet to see if such impertinence would be allowed.

A sense of shared style, declared the Lesser Tada, undaunted, a sense of urban polish appreciated – *that* is what the modern pleasure-seeker requires.

Oyuki and Ohasu had been acquired by the House of the Lesser Tada at roughly the same time and were thought of as a set. Neither had as yet acquired a sponsoring patron, and their reluctance to commit to dependency bonds was in itself considered a sign of modern times. You see the shape of it yet? said the Lesser Tada. Novelty is what attracts customers in Edo today, new words to old melodies...

Such chatter! Oyuki stood abruptly and poured a final bucketful of rinsing water down the shiny pink slope of her belly. But if you ask me, it's all scabbard and no blade. And she crossed over to the soaking trough then perched on the edge of it, swinging her legs around and into the water, first one, then the other.

Under the same roof, pleasure providers also are sleeping: bushclover and the moon.

HE SEEMS FOND of you.

Creating fondness was their occupation.

His was not sincere?

It is, said Ohasu shyly. As was that of the greedy baby for his mother's teats.

Hunting bats flickered in the twilight sky, and paper stand lanterns positioned under the eaves of the back veranda glowed softly, creating pools of light for those who wished to linger after the evening meal. And your friend hopes to buy back her contract?

The wine cups used by the Lesser Tada and Oyuki had been left on the low tray table, and Ohasu rinsed them like a host anticipating the arrival of more guests. They let her have her dreams. Let both of us dream. Since the funds advanced to purchase our robes and sashes are sufficient to keep us in debt.

The wind had risen, and the peony girl and the *haikai* poet watched as the evening rain began arriving in the summer trees on the hill slopes beyond the veranda.

I'm the sombre one, said Ohasu. The literate one. The one who is appreciated by older men, and by those who wish to display their understanding of the ways of the past. She picked up the wine flask and poured for Old Master Bashō then filled her own cup again. Many of my evenings are spent playing the poem cards game. Or matching seashells. Or folding paper cranes. This one old fellow brings out his collection of iris rhizomes every winter, and we pair them like for like.

Old Master Bashō smiled. Irises. But he was gazing out at the roiling trees, the first scent of rain in the dust already and the sound of it rattling in the leaves.

But the rhizomes only, said Ohasu. Never the flowers.

Ohasu opened the tobacco box. She offered her long bamboo pipe to the Old Master, who declined, then filled the tiny bowl with a pinch packed in tightly. Some men promise to visit me but I know they won't. Others make promises and always come. Yet I wait equally for those who appear and those who don't. She plucked a shard of coal out of the brazier and lit her pipe then sucked in the smoke and exhaled it. Oyuki strives for guests because she believes she can redeem her contract. But I don't have her strength. Or her credulity. Ohasu tapped the pipe bowl on the rim of the ash tube, dislodging the pellet of charred tobacco. And I prefer those who fail to keep their promises.

The sky cracked open along a splintering seam of silver, the rain swung in on them; and they pulled their tray tables and floor cushions back under the eaves, pleased with the suddenness of the downpour.

Some of the older ones are sad, Ohasu said. They wish to extend the joys of spring but cannot manage it. She shot a quick glance at the old poet, as if to confirm that he was not offended by her candour. I have my skills. Yet, nevertheless, disappointments occur. Some men become angry. Some become morose and drunk and fall asleep – them I cherish. Some try bear's gall bladder or Korean ginseng or a potion of dried tiger penis. They take their doses then sit facing me with an expression of self-concentration, fingering their limp little man-twigs hopefully. Some find what pleasures they can in hurting me. I am not to be wounded or bruised, but there are those who understand how to create pain that leaves no marks. Them I try to avoid. Some men wish only to suckle me, and although no milk flows I give the nipple willingly and calm them until they sleep. Some difficult types wish to create complications and demand two or three of us rolled together like dumplings, and some wish to include a pretty boy too so as to have available all the slippery gates of love. And some say they wish to discover a new configuration, a complexity of arousal that has never before been attempted. But for them there can be only disappointments, for all things have been done. She regarded Old Master Bashō coolly for a moment then said it again, All things.

The peony girl reloaded her pipe and lit it with a coal like a glowing tooth, sucking the smoke up in two quick gasps then tapping the bowl empty.

But shouldn't I wish for something for myself? Isn't there somewhere that I should place my hopes? It's a question for which I have no answer. So I pour wine and sing and dance and chat and play finger games. And when special requests have been negotiated and extra fees paid, magpies build bridges and I wait where I am told and do whatever is required.

The wind came up in an abrupt rush that flung a wet spray deeper onto the veranda, and they scrambled to get farther back under the eaves, laughing at their own agitation.

'A sudden evening shower,' Ohasu recited, 'and the ducks run around the house quacking.'

The old poet smiled. Did you write that?

I tried it another way too. 'A sudden evening shower, and a solitary woman sits gazing pensively.' But that seems too sentimental to me.

Old Master Bashō picked up his cup and sipped at it. Your 'gazing pensively' stanza would be easy to link to. You could use it to connect a poem on love to one on the summer rain.

Perhaps, said Ohasu. Yet, still, it seems too obvious.

And the 'ducks' stanza is lighter, I suppose. He sat watching the rain lashing the trees then said, But it's within the link itself that beauty lies, the interval between two stanzas.

Not in the words?

No. In what jumps across from one stanza to the next and spans the gap. Our method is found in the art of collaboration. Poets sitting in a room composing a sequence together. Each voice pushing off from the one before.

I like the stanzas, Ohasu said.

So do I. It's what blocks me.

Do your followers appreciate the distinction?

Some do. Most don't. He turned towards her and said, Most are like those of you who live in the floating world of desire, drifting along like clumps of river foam, accepting every occurrence as it arrives.

And is that how you see us?

Old Master Bashō said nothing.

But I suppose it's true. I am indeed a fashion. Ohasu loosened her bodice and pulled it open for the cooling she might find. A father is unable to pay his debts, and a small girl is sold to a pleasure provider in Edo. A city man is sent as his agent. He ties a rice-straw rope around the girl's waist and leads her out through a village emptied of its people, for no one there wishes to see the shame of the girl who is the one selected to be sold. The girl wept the night before but now her eyes are dry. She doesn't gaze about to remember the world of childhood she will never again see. Her mother calls and she looks back. But there is nothing for her to say and nothing to do, and the small girl walks away doubting that she will ever see her home again.

The morning sun warms them and steam from tilled fields rises in silver clouds of moist air. Her mother has not prepared a travel bundle for the girl because there was nothing she could be given. Her hands are empty. They hang at her sides. She doesn't even grasp the rope which connects her to the city man plodding along before her, and when he turns off the road and finds a secluded dell with a boulder the size and shape of a kneeling cow she lies on it on her belly with her robes bundled up around her middle and her legs pried apart so that her little jade gate is exposed. Does she still remember the feel of the city man's breath on her bare skin? The sound of the slap of his hand rubbing up the red wad of his man-parts?

No. Because she wasn't there. The trees were there, the rocks and grasses and insects were there, as were the bird-calls and flecks of sunlight and shifting breeze. But the small girl was absent. She didn't hear the city man snuffling in his lust. Nor did she smell the crushed ferns at her feet, nor feel the gritty surface of the rock she was lying on. Look at me, the city man croaked finally, look at me now. But the girl wasn't there so she made no response to the stinking mucus splattering on the backs of her thighs.

It had happened. But it had not happened to her.

Do you understand why I'm telling you this? Ohasu picked up her long pipe again. Such absences are for me my intervals.

The old poet sat in silence beside her.

And yet it is in the telling of such things that I connect together my intervals. So perhaps that is why I find comfort in stories, in the shapes and sounds of the words as well as their meanings.

There's no real comfort there.

No? Ohasu poured for Old Master Bashō then poured for herself. When Oyuki and I were brought into the pleasure quarters, we were children who were permitted only to obey. When we cried, we were told to stop crying, and when we asked to go home, we were told we had no homes to return to.

All must bear their lives.

I would have preferred mine otherwise. Ohasu took up her wine cup and drank then set it back on the tray table with a sharp click. Tell me, she said, why should there be no solace for women like me? Can you in your black sleeves explain that?

Old Master Bashō regarded her for a moment then said, There's no answer for such a question.

No? 'My love-passions flame up but in my breast my heart chars.' Ohasu poured for her guest and poured for herself then said, A useless indulgence, I suppose. Yet those words were written by a woman who felt what I feel, and they do seem to offer me comfort. The *words*, she repeated, are what comfort me.

Old Master Bashō looked at her again, studying the small woman sitting stubbornly beside him, then he returned his attention to the thunderstorm raking the trees, the rain thrusting downward in broad swinging sheets, the world closing down within the turbulence of the gathering of its darkness.

The white poppy: wings torn off a butterfly as a keepsake.

SHE ASKED HIM WHY HE was so dissatisfied.

Perhaps on another occasion I can explain it.

She said she wasn't sleepy. And he heard a soft rustling as she crept around the folding screen that divided the shared room, her small body pale in the humid darkness. Tell me now.

I tried before...

Try again.

He lay waiting in the sweltering darkness then said, The yearning to describe an instant of beauty is a habit difficult to overcome. As is the wish to have what you make seem true. And important. Because then you're doing it for others. And therefore it's theirs, not yours. And only if it's yours can you release it.

For others to link to?

Yes. To complete.

She leaned forward to be nearer. And that's the goal? To free yourself of solitude?

Old Master Bashō did not answer at first, unsure how to respond and trusting that she would listen to what he said and understand what he meant so that he had to be certain he believed it himself. There are mosquitoes still. Come in under the net.

She slipped in quickly and lay beside him at the edge of his quilt.

He told her that penetrating into the beauty of the true nature of things had been the goal of the poets of the past, and that he himself had struggled to achieve it. But no longer. It is the ordinary that seems satisfying to me now. And not the ordinary seen in new ways, but the ordinary as it is, the ordinary linked to the ordinary.

So it does become the leap across? Not the idea, but the connection? I wonder if your followers can understand that. Ohasu lay on her belly with her bare shoulders raised, supported by her forearms. So a summer night *becomes* the scent of its orange blossoms, and that in itself is enough…

He followed her down the corridor and out to the thermal bath in the garden, the summer moon's radiance silvering her small body. She removed the boards fitted over the trough then slipped into the heated water like an otter down its slide.

Say you saw something, said Ohasu, a flower in the mist, a bright winter bird, an insect singing in cut brushwood, and you made a stanza about it in such a way that the connection was between the thing itself and your version of it.

Old Master Bashō smiled. I see you wish to defend those who write stand-alone haiku.

Just that you could do that.

And would you wish to spend your life making things out of words then sticking them up on walls?

Ohasu adjusted the cloth protecting her coiffure then stood dripping and perched on the outside edge of the tub, gazing out at the silver and black shapes of the mountains and trees in the moonlight. It would be odd for a girl, I know. But I've always loved words, the shapes of them.

Old Master Bashō eased himself up out of the hot water too.

The character for horse, you can see his four little legs running. And the word for flying looks like birds on the wing.

Most aren't pictures.

No, I know. But words had been like a magic world for Ohasu as a child, a peach blossoms spring she could climb down into and take possession of. The shapes of words were paths she could trace out, following them this way and that; they were mazes to study and admire, maps and diagrams and arcane charts, each new one a delight. It's still that way for me, Ohasu said. And the old fellows who come out to visit me know it. Obscure words for rare flowers, odd names for lost cities, weird-beings that are no longer thought to exist, they write them out and show me how to write them, and each becomes something we share. Is that not a form of linking?

No doubt. But your house master will still want to be paid in cash money.

Yes. That's so. For all his foolish chatter about romantic love. Ohasu stood abruptly and climbed out of the soaking trough then stepped into her clogs. She went out into the garden then turned to face him, her wet body sleek in the moonlight. Is his way of linking so very different from yours? When something occurs to you, an image, a phrase, an idea, and you jot it down and think about it and try it different ways, what are you linking to if not another, earlier attempt at the same thing? Your links are to yourself. Ohasu unwound the white cloth from around her hair and began wiping herself dry with it. So why shouldn't mine be? Why shouldn't I try to make things out of words even as others are trying make something out of me?

Perhaps you should. But doing it on your own seems too lonely.

I am seldom on my own, said Ohasu. But I'm always alone. She finished wiping down her legs then wrung out her little white cloth and held it draped over her belly in a belated gesture of improvised modesty. Didn't you like my story about the weepy little girl? My listeners always find it moving. Because they are willing to believe that I have no choice in what I do. And in what is done to me.

Old Master Bashō said nothing. And when they returned finally to their shared room, each wondered which side of the folding screen the peony girl would choose and which would be the other's preference.

The Pariah Supervisor
非 人 長

He blindfolded the arsonist then led him down into the dry riverbed.

The Edo city constable and his men were arrayed along one edge of the execution grounds, hunched like jackdaws in their thick winter robes.

I will show you a rare occurrence, said the supervisor.

Your demonstration is unnecessary. All acknowledge your skills. What we cannot tolerate is your person.

The cold had no effect on the pariah supervisor; and he was wearing only a cuirass of pink and purple leather scales studded with steel rivets, the monstrous expanse of it curving out over the swollen bag of his immense badger-belly in a manner that offended the constabulary men, as did the heavily-oiled mass of his chignon riding on the roll of fat on the back of his neck and leaving streaks of grease there.

I said we don't need to see this. We know what you can do.

You don't know what I can do.

The arsonist waited, shivering in fear, his bound head tilted off to one side like someone listening for faint sounds coming from afar. He had burned down the house of a moneylender to whom he was indebted, hoping to destroy both the man and his account books. They had survived, but the building and its neighbours were lost to the conflagration; and in a city of flimsy wooden structures with paper doors and straw floor mats, there could be only one punishment for such a crime.

The arsonist said he needed a moment to compose himself. But his robe was being stripped off his shoulders like the prelude for the bedding of a new bride, his arms lifted out of their sleeves, first one then the other, and his sash too pushed down until the wad of garments hung low on his hips much in the style of happy-day dancers responding excessively to heat and wine and the cries of their fellows.

Don't move.

But I'm not ready…

Don't move.

The supervisor took his position behind him. He had a stiff-blade chopper, heavier than most, one with an oversized hilt further thickened by a layer of horse-hide held in place by windings of copper wire, the coils of which crisscrossed over each other forming diamond-shaped lozenges that improved the gripping surface and added what he considered to be an aesthetic component.

The arsonist declared in a quavering voice that he thought more might be learned from his case, a cautionary lesson that could help others avoid the mistakes he himself had made. He said he thought some kind of confession might be composed, the truth captured in vivid language, words blazing with authenticity, the credibility that of a man whose life was ending so that the value of the honesty of the document thus obtained more than compensated for the slight delay that would be required; but the supervisor took a step back, set his feet with his knees slightly bent then drove forward off his plant-leg, rotating his hips as he hit through, swinging across low and hard and flat, and with both arms fully extended at the point of impact so that the arsonist flipped apart in an explosion of entrails that leapt into the icy air like flung eels.

The supervisor stood between the two halves of the dying body, the spray of fresh offal steaming on the frozen earth. That's a thing it is said cannot be done to a standing man. But as you have seen, I can do it.

The city constable stared at the sundered corpse, his face pinched shut with disgust. What do you want?

The arsonist's loin cloth had come apart with his destruction, and the supervisor plucked up one end of it then wiped clean his blade. To be included among those who enforce the laws of the shogunate.

To be included? The city constable looked at his junior officers; but it was their own fear of this non-person that had precipitated the difficulty, their sense that he was impinging upon them and blighting their prospects. It's impossible.

The blood flow had reached his sandals, but the supervisor made no attempt to evade it.

Don't ask for what can never be given.

The pariah supervisor remained as he was.

Never! cried the city constable. Never! You have no

family, no registry, nothing to certify you. He glanced at his men again, but there would be no help from any of them. You're not a person. You have no name.

I am called Jirobei the Supervisor. As you know.

Called by whom?

All who encounter me.

And you think that's enough?

It's what I'm called.

The city constable again glared at those who were aligned with him, brazier-lovers, cushion-choosers, men gone soft on the generosity of the shogunate. Don't ask to be included, he said. Ask for something else.

There is nothing else. The supervisor waited then said, I need permission to go inside buildings. I need permission to ask questions and require answers. This city is growing; malcontents are arriving, unruly types with eager fingers. He studied the row of constabulary officers looking back at him helplessly. I need permission to hurt others. Hurt artisans and tradesmen and teachers. Hurt samurai.

Not samurai.

The supervisor waited.

There's no person in this world who would approve that. Never.

I can't serve you if I am not allowed inside your buildings. The huge man smiled to himself then said, Typical urban habitations, savouring the sound of each word as he pronounced it, the lovely feel of it on his lips.

Your service is not required.

The blood that had reached the supervisor's rice-straw sandals pooled there but went no farther. You haven't appreciated that urban poverty responds best to harsh methods, Jirobei said.

Why do you care about the poor?

I don't care about them. I care about orderliness.

There's no reason for you to pursue such matters. Stick to your tallow vats!

There is no reason for anything. Other than in the doing of it.

HE KNEW THERE WERE seasonal dances but had never seen them performed. Special foods were eaten – little cakes filled with sweet red bean paste being a particular delicacy – but he himself had not tasted them. Residents of the city came out into moorlands to view the flowering cherries, but they would never venture near the pariah encampment nor even look in its direction. Jirobei acknowledged their loathing and accepted it; and if their songs in praise of the shell-pink clouds of cherry blossoms were not meant for his ears, he heard them anyway.

The huge man had a house of his own now, a cottage allocated in recognition of the new duties he had finally been granted. It was at the edge of the rendering grounds where cart horses and dray oxen were processed after death; but he found no source of complaint in this location since for him, the stench of hacked animal parts boiling in iron vats brought back fond memories of home.

Jirobei had never needed much sleep; now he

needed even less. He had adopted the habit of strolling into the shogun's metropolis at odd times during the night or day, wearing a cotton robe printed all over with oversized hibiscus flowers in cinnabar and indigo, a bold design that he considered flattering to his physique. He felt the sap of the world rising up through him. It left him agitated, unsettled, stimulated, at one with the new green of leaves unfurling on the city's hardwoods and the dewy freshness of fern shoots sprouting in the surrounding moorlands.

The pariah supervisor had been slashed in the face during an altercation with a gang of easy-way boys. The wounds had healed leaving a striae of scars that remained dead white despite his usual ruddy complexion, and the rictus crimping his upper lip meant that effort was required now for the supervisor to form words properly. For all that, Jirobei didn't regret this debility. He accepted what had been done to him in the same way he accepted what he did to others. And there were those who said that on very quiet nights, echoes of the howls of the easy-way boys could still be heard faintly reverberating, so deeply had the duration and complexity of their agony been soaked into the fabric of the shogun's city.

But the season of cherry blossoms filled Jirobei with a new restlessness. He bathed daily now, usually just at the blades of dawn, and he cleaned his teeth, scraped the dirt and dried blood out from under his fingernails, and wiped himself carefully each time after shitting. Everywhere were instances of regeneration to be embraced and extended; and the pariah supervisor welcomed it all, sitting naked and alone as the rising sun found the knackery and managing his long black hair, combing it out with a hand-cut boxwood comb then dressing it with camellia oil – much too heavily, he knew, but the pleasure of the scent was difficult to resist, as was his pleasure at adding an extravagant binding cord to hold his grossly oiled topknot in place – cherry pink, in honour of the season.

Jirobei was born from a misogynist's spasm. His father had been a large and angry man who possessed an unmatched ability to pull down other men and throw them aside. In his prime, he was seldom defeated although his victories were never praised. And as he aged and slowed and thickened, younger men learned to evade his arms and dance around him. He was beaten sometimes, and his bitterness at these losses was met with laughter and joy.

Jirobei's father had washed ashore as a boy and been raised among them, but his true origins were other and he was deemed unacceptable. Not of their blood, he could only marry a member of the despised non-human class of pariahs; and this humiliation created in his father a hatred of his wife and of women. Only the men whom he defeated or who defeated him found a grudging acceptance in his eyes, and only the moment of impact as two naked male torsos clashed together in the presence of spectators pleased him. He was nicknamed the 'Great White Bird' because of the paleness of his skin, and he had accepted that he would never earn love or respect. Rejection succoured him.

His first child – a small, sickly boy with the weasel-like face of his mother – had died after a year spent wrapped in hemp cloths that stunk of urine. But his second boy, large and ruddy, had from the moment of his birth given every indication of survival. Parts of him developed late, and it was only after a few months that they could hazard a certification of this sport's gender. He named him Jirobei – the 'second-born' – and he studied this boy as he grew and watched for the first hint of any trace of his mother in him. He found none. It was as if Jirobei had been formed wholly from his own flesh and had merely used his birth-mother as a passageway, with nothing of her adhering to him.

When the boy was old enough to totter about on his fat little legs, his father taught him how to unbalance other children by delivering sharp blows to the side of the head. And when the boy's legs became strong enough to support him and his growing belly in more aggressive manoeuvres, he taught him how repeated thrusting blows to the neck of an advancing child would stand him upright, limit his ability to counterattack, and ultimately topple him over. And when little Jirobei – hardly 'little' even at two and three years of age – was old enough to appreciate artfulness, he taught him how to land upon a defeated opponent and surreptitiously gouge his eyes or crush his testicles, doing it in such a manner that those watching would not notice while making certain that the screeching victim knew it was as intentional as it was unnecessary. You may one day have to fight him again, his father had told him, and he will remember what you did and so be constricted by the past even as you are attacking within the present.

Permission to enter residences had been rescinded due to complaints. But the roads and lanes and alleyways of the shogun's city remained available, and the pariah supervisor had developed the habit of lingering just outside the open widows and doorways of the homes of city-dwellers and watching as they occupied themselves with petty crafts and household chores. He would smile to himself benignly as they chatted together or dozed alone. He mused on the way they drank wine and smoked tobacco, the way they prepared food and ate it and fed their children, the way they laughed and sang, chanted sutras and called out curses, wept, squabbled and fucked; and he felt almost included, almost numbered among them, almost fully human.

One night he found himself outside the home of the arsonist he had punished, and he watched the man's widow until she spotted him and slapped the rain shutters closed. After that, he came often, choosing shadows and unanticipated vantage points. He became familiar with the men from the neighbourhood who visited the widow, men who would have been her husband's friends perhaps and now seemed hopeful of replacing him. Most drifted away as the cherry blossoms began falling, but a chandler who seemed intent on scratching his itch persisted so Jirobei made inquiries then visited him in his shop.

I guess you were waiting for me.

The chandler looked up from feeding the flames heating his wax pot.

Probably you heard that questions were being

asked about you. The huge man filled the shop's entryway, blocking out the milky spring sunlight. And surely you must have suspected that I would be visiting you. If not on one day, then on another.

Jirobei came inside and squatted in front of the chandler. His fat red thighs spread apart widely as he levered up his immense badger belly and rolled it forward, the pink and lavender leather strips of his cuirass creaking obscenely at the weight of the muscle and fat and tumid organs they were obliged to restrain. You have perhaps misunderstood the nature of mourning. You may have seen a woman's vulnerability as an opportunity for personal pleasure.

I, no, I haven't, I –

Don't. Jirobei held up one large red hand. Don't disrespect me.

The chandler looked back at him.

Dip your candles. Add the next layer.

The chandler took up the two hand-racks of dangling candles tied by their wicks and lowered them into the bubbling wax pot, holding them there then lifting them straight up so that the fresh layer would form smoothly.

Well. Then. A woman's husband dies. She feels lost, abandoned. What normal man wouldn't seek to take advantage of such a situation? To neglect to do so might even seem an anomaly. Jirobei savoured the lovely word on his lips then pronounced it again with exaggerated clarity: An anomaly.

I only think that people should –

No. Don't. You know what I'm asking. You know

what's required of you. You are the one that goes inside another man's house. You are the one who becomes aware of what happens there. Jirobei smiled at him. That layer is now dry.

But she invites me in...

That layer is dry. Dip your candles.

Some women have family members to help them, but she is alone...

I know that. And she will need soothing. Jirobei leaned closer to the gently bubbling liquid wax and thrust one thick red finger into it, holding it there, ignoring the pain or perhaps finding something of interest in it. Don't pretend that my request is unclear, said the supervisor. It is the violation of the dead man's home that concerns me. He removed his finger, newly pearlescent with a coating of hot wax, the skin at the rim where the wax sheath ended burned to a deeper shade of red than was usual for him. Do not misunderstand me.

The chandler lifted out his candle bunches with trembling hands. He spoke in awkward bursts, describing aspects of his life he thought exculpatory. Good deeds. Simple observations that others found useful. Poignant moments. Gifts. Alms. Insights on the true nature of things...

The chandler's voice died away as the supervisor continued shifting forward, the awful shape of him rising upward and inward, filling the small workroom with his bulk as he gently touched his burned and wax-coated finger to the man's lips to silence him. I asked you not to insult me by pretending that what I want is unclear.

The chandler looked up at him. I won't go there again. Ever.

Why?

Why? Because you want me not to...

Jirobei hung above him in a tumescent and silent red mass of disappointment.

Because I don't want to. It's my choice not to go. Mine.

THE ARSONIST'S WIFE HAD found sanctuary in the service of the Lady Aoi no Tsubo, an orphan of the imperial palace who was in residence in the shogun's city. She was taken on as a serving maid; and if her duties weren't onerous, they nevertheless required a certain resourcefulness, for the Lady Aoi was conducting a surreptitious love affair with the son of a senior retainer of the Tokugawa Shogunate. Such illicit unions between the original court aristocracy and the new warrior class of the samurai were forbidden; but the Lady Aoi was a woman susceptible to desire, and she used the arsonist's wife to carry messages to her lover and arrange trysts.

If the arsonist's wife feared the repercussions of betrayal, she feared the pariah supervisor more; and one hot summer night, it was Jirobei who stepped out of the shadows at a deserted mansion as the young Hori samurai arrived for his night of summer moonlight and love.

She's not coming, Jirobei told him.

All the gates to the mansion were still sealed, and the young Hori samurai had been caught exposed in the open roadway. He circled to the right, his sword held in a forward-parry position, light from the round moon glinting on the curved steel of the blade.

The pariah supervisor held out both his arms to show that he carried no weapons. He told the young samurai that violations were unacceptable; and although rash acts committed in the throes of love would hardly seem to pose any threat to the shogunate, even the slightest disobedience, if allowed to go unpunished, could result eventually in the collapse of the Tokugawa family and the destruction of all they had achieved.

I myself am not permitted to hurt you, Jirobei said. But my duty requires me to present you to those who will.

Jirobei told him he knew that samurai believed some deaths were honourable and some weren't. He understood that samurai prized being in control of the manner of their own death even more than they did the right to take the life of another person. He said he had no opinion on such matters. But he wondered if the distinction wasn't without merit.

The young Hori samurai reached the wall of the enclosure and continued to move along it for want of any better strategy. He could see the shape of his adversary in the middle of the moon-washed summer road, his naked red flesh shiny with perspiration and his awful body armour like an immense tumour that was the colour and consistency of fresh viscera. But his face was shadowy and his eyes two black holes.

One man might die in a fight with a sword in his hand, Jirobei said, while another man died squeezed by an illness that wrung him like a wet cloth. Yet there are also those who die in their sleep peacefully under soft quilts, or drift away with the chanting of the *nembutsu* in their ears. He wondered if the manner of it really mattered. Death was death. Wasn't all else embellishment? Jirobei told him that he himself accepted death as a gateway. He believed that each life led to the next through death's blessing, and that how one behaved now would determine the place one occupied then. Jirobei's voice was calm, discursive, compelling. He came closer as he spoke, and he told the young swordsman that although he himself had been born a foul blot staining the earth, he had nevertheless risen through his own merit to a position just under that of fully human so that hardly more than the width of a gnat's leg still separated him from them. He told him he accepted his karma. He awoke each morning as he had slept the night before. He found no pleasure in wine. Food was no beguilement. He took no interest in carnal release, neither the holes of women nor those of boys drew him. When money was offered he passed it on to others. He himself owned nothing that hadn't been scavenged from a dead man or one dying or about to die. He accepted that he would have no legacy, no future, no wife or child to mourn him. Nor had he ever even considered the possibility of attempting such an arrangement, nor would he.

But that did not mean he lacked feelings.

And it did not mean he lacked hope.

Jirobei continued advancing slowly, calmly, his palms held out empty before him like a drought-farmer praising the arrival of summer rain. He told the young

Hori samurai that he had discovered his single purpose, his one treasure, and that its possession was why
he was still alive. He told him he had been slashed and
stabbed, struck by cudgels and rocks and iron batons;
he had been hit by arrows and lead bullets and cross-
bow bolts. He had been burned in a fire and he had
been drowned in a pool. He had been dragged behind a
horse once and strangled once with a twisted-rope gar-
rotte that left marks on his neck. He had been hung naked from the side of a gate and left there to die in the
summer sun by men who were too afraid of him to stay
and watch it happen. And he had not died, Jirobei said
as he came closer, speaking calmly, soothingly. Because
he had his single purpose, his one precious desire. The
metal of blades could not kill him before this goal was
achieved, nor could the wood of cudgels, nor the earth
he was dragged over. He had survived the heat of the
pyre's flames, the rise into the air from the knot of a
hangman's noose, and the descent through blue water
to the darkness at the bottom because of his one perfect
singularity.

Jirobei had arrived close enough for the young Hori
samurai to cut him but the boy couldn't do it, not even
as the wedge-shaped tip of his sword blade was forced
up against the out-thrust curve of the pariah supervisor's immense badger-belly, pushed higher and higher
until it rested just under the thick red flesh of his throat.

My one desire, my one purpose, is to be reborn as a
fully-human child. A little baby boy or baby girl. Small,
pink, helpless, loved. My one desire is to suckle a human
mother's teat and grow healthy and strong. Can there be

any greater thing to share? My singularity is my wish to return. Again and again and again. And to be you.

Jirobei removed the sword from the young samurai's grasp. They're waiting for us, he said. He turned him around and placed one large red hand on the back of his neck, feeling the bones there, owning them. It's not far. We'll be there well before dawn.

NO RAIN FELL.

Dung from dogs and dray beasts dried in the sun, and rose in great choking clouds of faecal dust that swirled throughout the shogun's city in a foul miasma. It was an awful season. Residents ventured outdoors with dampened scarfs wound around their faces, red-rimmed eyes peering out fretfully through the narrowest of openings. Duties were neglected, punishments cancelled, celebrations allowed to wither into insignificance. It was a time for remorse, a time of drought and contagion; and at the height of the worst of it, the pariah supervisor departed from Edo, the carry-sack slung over his shoulder containing the cutters and choppers and other tools he required. His scavengers had watched him don his cuirass and said not a word. The supervisor chose an oak cudgel with iron ferrules on each end that were the size and shape of a human eye socket, and the sound this staff made on the dry ground as he walked reassured him with the certainty of his passage. Extra sandals dangled from his obi sash, as did a water gourd and a sash-pouch containing various items: a little claw-hook for working in tight spaces, a focusing lens in a protective flat-sack, a shard of obsidian glass sharper than any knife, and a flint and steel for cloudy-day fires. The supervisor had developed an appreciation of the pleasure people found in personal possessions, and he also carried with him a few pretty seashells, a string of amber beads, and a few exotic coins; he had a set of brass buttons that had been cut off the naval jacket of a butter-eater by the mob that had smothered him, the idea of the feared invader reminding him of his father; he had a pair of lead bullets that he'd dug out of his own flesh himself and retained in commemoration of the accomplishment; he had a double-handful of keepsake teeth and a few ornamental knots of dried skin cleverly configured; and wrapped in a cup of mulberry paper was the petrified skull of a shrew-mole, an ancient artefact that was decorated all over with archaic and mysterious writing for which he hoped one day to find a reader.

The under-constable at Shinjuku New Station sat on his horse and watched the approach of the huge, dust-covered creature wearing body armour that was as gaudy as fresh entrails. He hated seeing him. He hated the way his massive red arms and shoulders and buttocks and thighs were exposed, hated the nakedness of his flat red face, the scarring there. The under-constable's disgust and fear settled itself most intensely upon the supervisor's flamboyant hairstyle, the great folded excrescence of night-berry blackness grossly oiled and configured into an exaggerated display never before seen, the excess of it certainly meant to be an affront.

You are not permitted to stay here. The under-constable carried a stabbing spear, and he held it at a provocative angle. Not to eat nor to rest. And certainly not to sleep overnight.

The pariah supervisor halted in front of him. The day was warm. Autumn insects filled the slanting orange afternoon light, and in the distance could be heard the steady rasp of a soybean grinder.

Shinjuku New Station was a starting point for journeys to the west, and shops and sheds lined the road, the cheap inns and noodle stalls and dray stables and brothels intended for the use of those heading out of the city. Carters and draymen sprawled at their ease on the roadside benches of wine shops or squatted near the blacksmith's forge and watched him at his labours, as if the fact of work occurring was in itself of interest to them.

You have made a mistake, the pariah supervisor said, forming his words with care. For I don't wish to stay here. He stood in the dust of the road with his carry-sack slung over one shoulder, each of the hacking tools it contained wrapped within individual hemp-cloth pouches to muffle the rattle of metal against metal; and he lifted his thick red forearms and rested them across the iron top-knob of his cudgel, placing first one there then the other like a butcher balancing the skinned carcasses of slaughtered dogs. I respect the law, Jirobei said. And I acknowledge the requirements of those who administer it. He lowered his eyes modestly. For I number myself among you.

There had been a carp pond at Shinjuku New Station once, stocked with fry in the expectation of an effortless profit. But the pond had become choked with water-weeds, the young fish died; and their bodies had rotted on the pond banks, leaving only a lush clotting of reeds, home now to frogs and the snakes that hunted them. The dried reeds could have been collected and woven into the surface sheets used for tatami mats. But the disappointed fish-farmers didn't harvest them; and the reeds grew to the edge of the roadway and collapsed under the accumulation of their own weight so that the under-constable's horse danced nervously on a crackling carpet of dry stalks.

The pariah supervisor circumambulated the dead pond. He paused for a moment like a man listening for the sound of the autumn wind then crossed over to the blacksmith's furnace. Those squatting there got up deferentially. They moved aside, seeking to tuck in behind one another with the awkward uncertainty of disturbed sheep.

Jirobei stood looking at the fire. Then he put his hand into the tossing flames at the forge mouth. He held it there and held it there then removed it.

The blacksmith backed away as if he himself had been burned, and the carters and draymen adopted the worried solemnity of men who realise that they might have to defend suppositions they no longer trusted.

You can live three ways. Jirobei held up his swollen red hand, as if in confirmation of the linkage between what he did and what he experienced as being done. You can be told of a thing like a flame. And recognise what the words mean. How they fit together. And so use your understanding as a guide. This is called the way of the learner of easy lessons. Such a person knows how to describe a flame. And nothing more.

Or you can choose to stand close to a flame and observe it with your own eyes. Study its colour, its dance, the heat it provides, the shapeless shape of it in its wavering. And through such an effort come to know the meaning of flames. This is the way of the satisfied seeker. He can use flames but will never himself become part of any fire.

But then there is the third way. My way. To reach out and be burned by it. And only if you can accept this third way can you understand the true soul of a flame. My way is the way of the one who always arrives. And you cannot bear to know what that entails.

Arrives? Arrives? The under-constable's voice cracked like a duck pelted by gravel. You aren't even permitted to be here! he cried; and his horse began prancing sideways, kicking out at the loose reeds dressing the roadway.

The supervisor observed the under-constable. You're poor at this.

The under-constable jerked his horse around and brought it under control again, as if doing that much might return him to where he wished to be.

Because you're afraid. But don't you understand that if I'd wished to harm you, it would have happened already?

The under-constable sat on his horse with his spear in his hand and did not respond or move in any way.

Your death owns you. As mine owns me. Only by accepting this can you live in the world.

The under-constable waited, his jaw working like that of a man chewing a tough knot of gristle.

Go home, the pariah supervisor said. If you have a child, cuddle it. If you have a wife, compliment her. And if your aged parents are still with you, ask them about their lives and listen to what they say. Own what you have. And be satisfied with it.

He stood for a moment longer then turned away and continued on through the hamlet and out onto the road west.

Winter Seclusion

冬 籠 り

They were cold. And they were tired. And after reaching the half-way point, they had foundered on *Night rain at the barrier gate, and along this road walks no one*, an image that seemed to offer no way out of the gloom they had created for themselves.

The white paper doors still glowed with the last of the reflected snow light; but the Plantain Gate poets sat buried in shadows like an assembly of funerary sentinels, pondering options and sifting through precedents. Some moved their lips, others tapped fingertips or folded fans against the cold floor mats, checking rhythm against syllable-count, and a few, deep in thought or chilled into stupefaction, stared blankly at nothing.

The session scribe offered to read back the sequence from the beginning, but Old Master Bashō said no. If they couldn't recall their arrival, how could they hope to fashion a departure?

Although they had heard this criticism before – usually in the same or similar terms – the linking poets configured their faces in the manner of thoughtful persons who find themselves confronting unexpected information, delaying, for the moment at least, the burden of the necessity of responding.

Whatever their teacher possessed was provided by them. Rolls of cotton cloth or silk cloth were left on his veranda, and writing paper and ink sticks added to the supply on his alcove shelf. The Old Master would find sacks of rice dumped into his rice bin, pickled vegetables stored in his larder, and packets of tea poured into his tea caddy. Before formal group sessions, a cask of rice wine would appear inside his entryway gate, trays of rice cakes topped with strips of pressed fish would be delivered, and afterwards, a few silver coins would be found tucked away discreetly in odd corners.

'Walks no one,' a voice intoned, 'along this road walks…'

'No one,' echoed another; but he too could do nothing with the bleakly austere stanza.

Then Little Ohasu, swaddled like a bagworm in a winter robe much too sombre for her profession and too large for her person, bowed formally, picked up her fan, and, her hand trembling in consternation and the cold, suggested a stanza:

'A moonless dawn; in the icy clarity of the mountain stream, fingerlings.'

The session scribe leaned forward to observe the shy peony girl kneeling demurely at the bottom of the room. She had never before spoken, much less attempted to add a stanza of her own. 'Along this road walks no one,' then, 'a moonless dawn…?' He turned questioningly towards Old Master Bashō. 'In the icy clarity of the mountain stream,' the session scribe recited tentatively, as if requesting a clarification. 'Fingerlings,' wasn't it? But the old man said nothing, and those around him sat staring straight ahead, draped within their thick winter robes, their fans lying untouched before them.

Ohasu picked up her fan again. Yes. To extend the emptiness of the road at the gate. But then to fill it in, add to it. So no moon. Because of the rain. And no sun yet either. But the first brightening of the dawn sky means the rain is ending. And with that light, you can see enough to have a sense of … of things beginning again. And it's … like that.

I see, said the session scribe. Fingerlings. And there would be a few of them, I suppose. So it moves the sequence from a tone of solitude to one of convergence. A nice change.

Ohasu shot him a quick glance of gratitude then lowered her eyes. But he was no ally, and she knew she didn't have one here.

The silk merchant picked up his fan. Kichiji was a large, well-fed man who had accumulated an immense fortune over the years and detected within his talent for shrewd business practices an overall excellence of perception. It is as I have always said, said the silk merchant, the energising faculty of the engaged imagination generates its own transcendent experience. One has been awake all night no doubt, sitting beside a mountain stream and musing on the beauty of the sadness of the nature of things, hearing the changeless change of deep water moving deeply, as if welling up from within the mountain's dark depths. Kichiji lifted his elegant fan then let it drop to his knee languidly, much in the way Old Master Bashō sometimes did. Then the far bank of the stream emerges from the shadowiness, as it were, and brings itself into one's consciousness gradually, gradually, like a butterfly fluttering out of an icy mist as it comes forward and –

How is a stream bank like a butterfly? asked Ohasu.

It is a metaphor, replied the silk merchant.

Yes? But which is for which?

Which for which?

Yes. Is the butterfly a metaphor for the stream bank? Or is the stream bank a metaphor for the butterfly?

Kichiji the silk merchant held himself upright for a moment, assembling the full magnitude of his dignity before lifting his fan again. The *image* comes into view *as if* released from the grip of the mountain's silence. And the trees and the rocks and the water grasses are still only patches of darkness, even as the surface of the water itself begins to become visible, gradually, gradually, and then within the icy water, one becomes aware of the ineffable *there*-ness of fish… He smiled in pleased agreement with himself. And so then thus, as it were, if I may say it, of the melancholy beauty of the burden of being.

I think it's simpler than that, said the session scribe; and someone else said, So do I.

Old Master Bashō remained silent, with his bald head tilted off to one side like an ancient and imperturbable tortoise. 'In the icy clarity of the mountain water, fingerlings,' he recited then said, a very good link.

Indeed it is, Kichiji said, always quick to agree with his teacher.

If, for example, Little Ohasu had chosen 'hatchlings' instead of 'fingerlings,' then the link would have been a failure.

The silk merchant returned the Old Master's gaze for a moment then looked away. Yes, he said uncertainly. No doubt that is the case of it.

No doubt. The question is why.

Yes. Why.

A powdery scree of snow crystals fanned out from where two of the white paper doors failed to close properly. The circle of linking poets sat pondering this distinction or pretending to ponder it, their breaths pluming out whitely in the frigid air and creating patterns like some bizarre form of signalling device. Old Master Bashō would not force a new link; nor would he do everything himself, for the method of his art was in the binding together of a group to create something that no one of them could have managed alone. If you don't understand why that image is the right choice, then how can you create a stanza that connects to it?

The linking poets sat with their heads down and their hands stuffed in their sleeves. Hatchlings? one said, and glanced around hopefully.

You praise the link but you don't understand it. So what is it that you're praising?

No one answered.

A crow alighted on a cedar bough in the garden, releasing a glittering fall of ice crystals that dropped from branch to branch in a susurrant cascade and landed with a wet plop on the snow surface below, the sound of it followed by its silence.

Perhaps our little dancing mouse will create a following link herself? suggested the silk merchant humorously. Since she seems to understand such things.

Such things? asked Ohasu.

Slimy things. His people-pointing finger arose obscenely erect. Wet slippery things.

Ohasu lowered her eyes, and stared at her empty hands cupped one inside the other.

Shall we abandon the sequence then? said Old Master Bashō. Was it too cold for them to continue? Did they want to go home?

No one spoke. A cooper's yard was next door, and the cooper's apprentices had begun splitting cedar planks into tub staves, the rhythmic sweep of their drawknives like the sound of silk gauze tearing. They had set a bonfire of scraps to warm themselves as they worked, and the scent of wood smoke drifting into the chilled room was like a reminder that sensible people sought comfort in winter.

Well, then, said the Old Master, perhaps that is as it must be. He would not save them. The formal winter session would be allowed to end as a failure.

Kichiji the silk merchant took up his fan again. The true path to an understanding of the art of the way of linking exists in the ability to perceive the subtlest of nuances. He nodded to himself, pleased with this stipulation. As the Old Master has explained, it is not the flower that is precious, nor the shadow of the flower, nor even the memory of the shadow of the flower, nor the yearning after that remembered shadow. No. Not that one. Nor that other. What must be captured is the *poignancy* of the memory of the yearning. And then, most precious of all, the sense of longing one feels for the loss of the soon-to-fade remembrance of that poignant yearning. Is that not what the Old Master has taught us?

No one replied. Steam rose soundlessly from the spout of the kettle, a frail, wavering line that broke apart before reaching the low ceiling.

Ohasu's hand trembled as she once again picked up her fan. Because hatchlings are so tiny? Isn't that the reason for it? Because the image would be too pathetic?

An appreciation of pathos emerges, murmured the silk merchant. Based on professional experience, no doubt.

Old Master Bashō said nothing, but he was watching as the session scribe picked up his fan. I believe the provisional female-member's idea is correct. Hatchlings under a cold, moonless dawn would have been too intense. It would stop the sequence. What is needed is a sense of hope. An affirmation. Her link is successful for that reason.

The Old Master waited for further comments then said, I agree. What could follow an image like 'hatchlings'? How could you build from it? But, 'in the icy clarity of the mountain water, fingerlings,' is just right. The water is cold, but the fingerlings will endure it. So too are the lives of men cold in this cold world. Yet we too must endure.

'Mountain stream,' said Ohasu, if it's not improper of me to insist on it; and Old Master Bashō looked at her, seeing the unwanted daughter, the child sold to the pleasure quarters for a debt, the girl who would never marry, never become a wife or a mother, her pinched little face pale in the frigid air, the rims of her nostrils pink with inflammation... 'A moonless dawn,' he recited. 'In the icy clarity of the mountain stream, fingerlings.' Sign it Ohasu. In kana.

The session scribe wrote out the stanza, his quick, fluid brush strokes like meadow swallows darting.

'A spray of plum blossoms as a disguise for his hat,' suggested one of the members, 'and the rustic lover makes his way over dewy moors.' Other ideas followed, each building on the one before; and afterwards Ohasu searched through the cold winter twilight clutching her precious copy of the completed sequence, her clogs rattling on the frozen road surface and her teeth chattering as she went from wineshop to wineshop until she found the rogue samurai Hasegawa, sitting alone as he always did now, morose and dishevelled and as lean as a wind-dried mackerel so that only his pair of fine swords in their black lacquer scabbards indicated he was something more than a common beggar.

Ohasu waited uncertainly in the entryway. She'd become familiar with the blankness of his stare without ever quite deciding how to respond to it. He was like a vagabond about to step onto a makeshift suspension bridge that he thought might not bear his weight; so she didn't tell him that she'd finally built up sufficient courage to suggest a stanza and it had been included in a formal sequence, didn't ask about his intentions for that evening or the night either but only said it was cold and she was tired and going home, and did he need any money?

Without merit but also without guilt: winter seclusion.

THE LOW ANGLE OF THE WEAK winter sun gave a slightly beige cast to the naked cherry trees in the pleasure quarters, as if the leafless branches were coated with fine particles of dust.

Ohasu counted syllables on her fingertips since there was no one to catch her doing it then jotted down on a sheet of waste paper:

Evening cherries at full-bloom within the evanescence of dust…

Next to that she wrote: *under the dust of evanescence.* Beneath it she added: *too delicate to survive the orange glow.* She studied both phrases then blotted them out. Too silly to survive being laughed at.

Ohasu sat behind the barred long-widow on the second floor of the assignations tea house with an extra robe draped around her shoulders. Poor old Hasegawa was off somewhere dunning welshers. He didn't like talking about it because he didn't like doing it. But better that than spending your evening in a wine pot.

She had guessed what he was before she knew his name. Her assignations teahouse employed loud-shouters who would harass debtors until the cash was produced, but they were cowardly bullies who wouldn't dare confront samurai so the Tada brothers had hired samurai of their own.

The peony girls had spotted Hasegawa Torakage waiting at the entryway portal, keeping to himself, clinging to the last shreds of his samurai pride. He was there the next day too and the day after that; and when they all came traipsing downstairs on their way to view the first colouring of the autumn leaves, there he was in the same place the same way. He had seemed dour even for a masterless samurai; and bold Oyuki had declared that if he was going to just sit there like an old mumbler, the least he could do was say his name so they'd know what to call out when they wanted to move him.

For his services, Hasegawa was paid a small fee based on the amounts he collected. He was fed and provided with wine – although never the best – and allowed to shelter in a small room just off the scullery. He explained later that he hadn't spoken because he didn't know what to say; and Ohasu had said, Well, you could have at least told us that.

I was afraid you'd laugh at me.

Oyuki laughs at everything.

But you don't?

No. I'm more selective.

Ohasu had decided to end her first attempt at a solo sequence with an image of vernal serenity: cherry trees in full bloom at sunset. But now that she had worked her way to the last stanza, the sight of the wintry trees in the frigid air made her uncertain. Wasn't there an equivalent tranquility in winter? Of course there was in reality, but in poetry? She would have asked Hasegawa except she was annoyed at him. She'd found a lovely padded robe to keep him warm, but he'd said he couldn't accept it. Why not? Because it has no family crests? No. Not because of that. He just couldn't. She'd left it in his cubby neatly folded. Probably it was still there. And he was out in the cold in his lightweight robe stuffing his hands in his sleeves.

Yet, still, when she cried, he tried to make her feel better; and when she was laughing, he tried to make her laugh more. So that meant something.

And the blossoms really *did* get dusty from the feet of strollers on dry days. So perhaps because the colour itself would appear drained away, as if exhausted by the need to ... to what? Respond to the beauty of the day? The colours *wearied* by it? Was she really capable of thinking that way?

Ohasu felt like throwing her writing-brush out the window. Was there no end to the stupidities that occurred to her? But you'd just have to go downstairs and pick it up again. And maybe he didn't feel the cold as long as he had a belly full of wine. But still ... flowers exhausted by their own beauty? Try telling that to him and see the pained look on his face as he struggled not to reveal what he thought of it.

Or, tell him to see it? Then fake a pouty face waiting as he tried to row back out into open water? There was a comedy to the squeamishness of the abandoned samurai, but it wasn't the kind you could laugh at. She knew he felt a solitude that she couldn't seem to compensate for. But that padded robe wasn't meant that way. So they were stuck because he was stuck, and she was stuck because they were; and she'd drink too much too, not to punish him or make him feel guilty, but just because sometimes she needed relief from the gloom of the shame of the warrior-servant with no master to obey. She would sing and dance with Oyuki and the others, laugh as they made townsmen bark like foxes or flap like chickens, all the while paying for the pleasure of being mocked while they did so. But in the cold light of mornings while they were waiting for the brazier to warm the room, she would watch Hasegawa watching her, and she would fill once again with sympathy and pity and dismay for the fact that he would never have what he wanted, all the while knowing that she herself could never be it. And then the room would finally be warm enough and they would start plotting how to sneak him back downstairs, and whatever should have been said hadn't been.

Ohasu corrected her brush tip, pondering colours and textures, blossoms and dust, only to become distracted by an outburst of love-shouting from down the hall. A grade-two back-worker was fucking a regular client Ohasu detested. Oyuki and the others had gone off to the bath, and she had stayed behind to finish her sequence only to become obliged to serve the unexpected arrivals, the repulsive client sitting on a stack of floor cushions and with his hand in his open robe, stroking up the red stump of his man-parts as if he thought she might become inflamed with desire at the sight.

Ohasu had distributed dishes of titbits and heated flasks of rice wine then checked the brazier and tossed in a few more chunks of charcoal. Will your honour require anything else?

The client had kept her waiting. What do you suggest? He was a sardine fertiliser merchant and the scent of it never quite left him.

That you enjoy yourselves leisurely. Ohasu had slid closed the door a little more firmly than was necessary then returned to her perch looking out over the lane.

Blossoms drained of their colour... But that had been said like that for hundreds and hundreds of years, the idea of blossoms yielding to their own transience. And poor old Hasegawa would point out that they didn't fade until after they had fallen, quoting old poets and commentators and explaining everything in detail when all you wanted was a simple yes or no. Was there a book he hadn't read? You could ask him would it rain tomorrow, and he would launch onto the history of the grades and degrees of the forms of falling moisture in ancient and modern poetry – fine mist, medium mist, heavy mist, drizzle, swinging rain, standing rain, sleet – on and on with this and that while you still had no idea if you should carry an umbrella. But then you'd also know he was doing it to fill the moment with words and so prevent any mention of things he couldn't bear to discuss except then he'd sneak in drunk late at night and not talk about anything else.

And yet the flowers *did* get dusty. And dustiness meant something.

So she wrote on her sheet of waste paper: *The blossoms at sunset, as they are in the dust of the world.* She looked at it then added: *The blossoms as they are at sunset,* repeating the phrasing to herself but not happy with any of it.

Going! Going! I'm going, squealed the grade-two; and the fertiliser magnate began bellowing it out too, as if her faking of sexual frenzy might be authenticated by a fraudulent demonstration of his own.

Ohasu checked back through her sequence of thirty-five stanzas, confirming that there were no awkward echoes. Hasegawa had said he thought she tried to get too much into each stanza, and she'd told him she thought he tried to do too little. But then he'd said later that what he meant was how you couldn't link to a stanza that was so dense; and she'd shot back, You mean *you* can't! as a tease; and he'd smiled and nodded and agreed that maybe that had been what he'd meant, and then stopped smiling and she knew that once again she'd somehow reminded him of the disgrace to his name.

The shouts down the hall had reached their crescendo – the absurd volume of it meant to suggest that great gouts of love were being splashed about the room – and Ohasu bent over her low table and forced herself not to hear it, working out other variations, '… of the dust of the world on the blossoms…,' the idea what she meant but the words tired. Perhaps she should come at it more directly? Say what a thing is and trust that the saying itself was sufficient?

Dusty blossoms at sunset, and the words for it also tired at the end of the day…

Something like that? The dust and the word 'dust?' Or was that too much like a novice trying to call attention to herself? Her sequence had to end with a mood of tranquility, matching the sense of quiet expectation it had begun with and thus bracketing the turbulent middle sections where –

Drawing dirty pictures? The sardine fertiliser client stood naked in her doorway, pulling up on his limp little man-stick to make it seem longer, his sack dangling, the slack maroon damsons deployed one below the other.

Is there something your honour needs?

What about what you need?

Ohasu looked past him out the door. The grade-two had followed him as far as the hallway, naked and shivering in the cold, her coif cocked off in a tangle as if she'd been dragged sideways through a hedge.

Is it more wine your honour requires?

How about you? A little wine help you relax?

I think younger sister is waiting for you. She looks disappointed. Did you have a misunderstanding? But surely it must have been a very *small* one, Ohasu said brightly; and the client turned away, penis-stub retracting, and stalked back to his room. Bring a cloth! And come do a wipe-up!

So, the moment between the orange warmth of sunset in spring and the first cool blues of the spring twilight. With the sun gone from the horizon but with its light still colouring the pale cherry blossoms, the orange of it filtering out their pinkness...

And the dust of the world ... the dust of the world...

That had to go away. Dust, the word 'dust,' the idea of it.

She regretted the loss then stopped regretting it; and she sat gazing down at Middle Lane, the leafless boughs of the cherry trees wet and black, the snow cleared away from the centre of the walkways but ridges of it dark with grime in the early twilight as groups of pleasure seekers began arriving, bundled up in winter robes against the cold, the samurai disguised in deep-brim basket hats or with head-cloths draped around cheeks and chins, some with their long swords hidden and some not, and the priests fooling no one by costuming themselves as doctors or scholars, and the townsmen with their faces exposed, oiled top-knots glistening, and here and there mixed in with them, a few peony girls in their gaudy robes, the hems showing, some wearing their oversized sashes in the manner of courtesans with front-tied sash-knots that could be detected under the drape of their winter cloaks, and others still costuming themselves more like serving maids...

Hasegawa was at the far corner, staring up at her window. He smiled when she saw that he had come back and put on his new robe. He held out both sleeves like a crane dancer and revolved through a circle to show himself to her then sketched a formal bow and continued on with wherever he was going. How lovely, Ohasu thought, despite the cold and the early darkness of a winter twilight, all of them lovely...

She spotted Oyuki and the others returning after their baths. They would be up here with their chatter soon. Pink at dawn so orange at sunset? She had told Hasegawa that she wanted to write about what her life was like. She knew such a topic was inappropriate for *haikai* poetry; yet he had surprised her by agreeing that a way might be found... But did the colour fade in the slanted light? Did it become muted?

The main entryway door was slapped open directly below her, and she heard them kicking off their clogs, bickering cheerfully about who got to use the inside privy and who had to go out to the communal facilities in the back garden.

Ohasu stared at the variations she had made then tossed aside the practice sheet. She loaded her brush, corrected the tip, and wrote:

The slanted orange light of the setting sun presses pinkness out of the last of the blossoms.

Why the 'last' blossoms?

But it sounded right, and in the margin at the end of her sheet she brushed the kana for 'o-ha-su' just as Oyuki slid open the door and cried, Are you *still* doing that?

The Emptiness Monk

虚 無 僧

It was too big. Koda cleaned the blood off and tried it on anyway. He could see well-enough through the looser weave at the front of the basket-hat, but he didn't like the way the bottom rim rested directly on his shoulders, blocking his lateral vision and making him vulnerable to attackers coming at him from the side.

I guess I'll just have to smell you first, he said to no one – to the cold empty air, the trampled and bloody snow, to the promise that each act finds in its execution a route to the next one.

He removed the basket-hat then pulled the Emptiness Monk's ink-black winter robe on over his own. It was too big too. There were bloodstains on the neck band, but he thought no one would notice. He wound the black obi sash around his shrunken belly.

Monks of Emptiness were a fighting order, and members were allowed to possess a single sword which they carried in a sack. Koda retrieved this monk's blade from where he'd dropped it and tossed it into the canal. He loaded his father's swords and his other gear into the black cloth sack and tied it across his back. He wrapped his too-long sword in the monk's leggings and slung it over his back too.

The monk's head had sunk to the bottom of the canal, but his corpse floated low in the water like a thing formed out of the coldness of winter itself.

Koda continued down the canal bank, his bad knee stiff again, that leg dragging and the off-side arm jerking in compensation. The road passed through a row of bone-white storehouses, the heavy wooden entry-doors set in thick walls and sheathed with iron plates icy with rime. Few people were out. Those he encountered hurried past, muffled up within winter robes. Shops and annexes were sealed against the frigid day, market stalls shuttered, the gate guards at residency blocks huddled around scrappy bonfires, on duty only for as long as fuel supplies lasted. Some looked up at Koda as he hobbled past and some didn't. It was too cold.

The berm road leading out to the pleasure quarters of Yoshiwara ran straight as a bowstring across an empty expanse of wild moorlands. Softly undulating snow fields stretched off in all directions under the cold membrane of stars, the whiteness there broken only by an occasional tangle of brambles or the leafless copses of alders or cottonwoods.

Koda slowed as he came to the first of the squalid wine shops and provisioners that had been established in the moorlands for the benefit of those who could not afford the Yoshiwara itself. Bonfires set in iron baskets on tripods burned in the middle of the road, and besotted celebrants staggered through the ragged fire-light as they went from wineshop to wineshop, some merry, some belligerent, some maudlin. One degenerate pair danced to a music heard only by themselves. A rascal with a goitre on his neck the size of a summer melon tried to show his penis to a woman who wouldn't look at it. Tucked off in odd corners here and there were true-style drinkers, cup-lovers who had levered themselves up onto the rim of a state of perfected incapability.

The Yoshiwara occupied a low rise of ground surrounded on all sides by empty moorlands. The dull white walls of the pleasure quarters were bleak and featureless in the frozen starlight; and Koda stood looking at it for a long moment then turned away and hobbled back into the berm-road hamlet, dragging his bad leg through the maze of alleys and waste grounds, following whichever road he happened to find himself on until he came to an abandoned wineshop with streaks of light showing where rain shutters were fitted imperfectly. He slid open the entryway door and stepped inside. A troop of gamblers had taken over the building. They'd built up the fire in the sunken fire pit and were stripping the interior, ripping out wooden fixtures and floorboards like wraiths of destruction and burning them.

We're closed for repairs, one of the gamblers said; and the others showed Koda faces solemn with malice.

Koda lifted off his basket hat but remained in the entryway.

A tall man sat alone on the single remaining floor mat. He had a solitary tray table with a wine flask and cup on it while the others shared a communal wine pot heating on a trivet set at the edge of their fire. A padded robe was draped loosely over the tall man's head and shoulders; and in the tossing shadows of the firelight, he looked like a moray eel peering out of its hole.

Koda saw that some of the ruffians were wearing the two swords of a samurai although the crests on their robe sleeves had been removed or defaced. You don't know where you are, said the tall man.

I guess not, Koda said.

Speak up, said the tall man. My hearing is poor. He shoved back the winter robe. Both his ears had been sliced off close to the skull, leaving only crimped buds of flesh, shiny pink as a newborn baby's lips.

I said I guess I don't where I am.

But it doesn't worry you.

No.

The man nodded to himself. There are thirty of us here. All armed and willing. He gazed around as if inviting a confirmation of this estimation. Does that not create a sense of anxiety?

Do I look anxious?

The tall man smiled. No. No you don't. So then you don't know who I am.

Koda said nothing.

You don't know of me?

Koda remained where he was just inside the door. I've heard of an easy-way gambler out here called Earless Gompatchi.

That's better. And what do you know of him?

Koda said nothing. He swung off his elongated carry-sack and leaned it against the entryway wall, the clank of the weapons inside sounding against the wooden pilaster. The gamblers had noticed the exaggerated hilt of the too-long sword protruding above his shoulder and knew that no monk would ever carry such a field-harvester.

Let me guess then. That the hero Gompatchi is fair in all things? Is that not it? Brave in street-brawls? Dauntless in love? A friend to the poor and a scourge on the rich? And a clever master of the new art of flower-card gambling?

Maybe that's it, Koda said.

Then perhaps you would like to tell me who you are.

Koda said nothing then he said, A cold person.

Earless Gompatchi smiled. A cold person? Nothing more?

A person alone.

I see. Then tell us about your holy vows.

My vows?

It's not permitted to wear the robes of an Emptiness Monk if one has not taken the vows of the order. Some might wonder if you are a true follower of the way. Some might accuse you of committing an impersonation.

Koda shifted the weight off his bad knee and continued to watch the man addressing him.

Where did you get your disguise?

I found it.

You found it. Earless Gompatchi smiled affably. So you met a monk who didn't need his robes and hat any longer?

Maybe that's it.

Why didn't he need them? Had he changed his way of life?

Koda said nothing.

I think you robbed him. Earless Gompatchi smiled

again then said, I think you attacked him and took his possessions unlawfully.

You can think whatever you like.

Earless Gompatchi sat musing for a moment then said, Listen to this. There was a difficulty a few years ago, one that could not be resolved, and my associates and I found ourselves condemned to severe punishments. One man lost his hands, another his feet, two were blinded. I was given a choice. The shogunate officers said they would cut off my ears and sever my man-parts. But if I could cut off my ears myself, the rest of me would be left intact. The knife they gave me had a dull blade. And even though I gripped myself tightly in my belly-spirit, the sound of the ear-sawing, the pain of it and the bleeding… He smiled at the recollection and said, Even if you can cut through one, the blood-seepage making your grip on the knife handle slippery, even if you can manage it, you still have the other, with all the pain of the one you just cut screaming at you and the memory of that pain and the anticipation of the new pain to come. Trust me, this is not a thing most men can do.

He moved his head from side to side again, displaying his ear buds.

But look how well I did it. Clean slices, friend, clean cuts both. First the left, then the right. So what do you say to that?

How do I know you still have your man-parts?

Gompatchi laughed and said, Very good! Come and sit by the fire and get warm.

Koda hung back for a moment then came forward and found a place among them. I'm a Koda, he said. Of the Koda of Dewa.

Dewa is far away.

Yes it is.

You also said you're alone.

Yes.

What did you mean? That you prefer the solitary life?

Koda looked at him. Just that it's how I am.

All right. Gompatchi had noticed the ulcerous wounds on his wrists, the damage done to his knees; and he asked if his tonsure hadn't been inflicted in the punishment gaol.

Something like that.

Samurai aren't usually treated so disrespectfully.

Koda said nothing.

My understanding is that samurai should be killed or forgiven, said Gompatchi, but never imprisoned. He referred the question to one of the samurai in his employ, a large, sombre man from the Ishida Clan whose drooping eyelids and heavy features gave the impression of someone saddened irrevocably by the difficulties of the world.

Or allowed to kill themselves, said the Ishida man.

Yes. Of course. Cut the belly like a good boy. Gompatchi looked at Koda. But that hasn't been your understanding of such matters?

I guess not, Koda said.

You guess not. Earless Gompatchi adopted a thoughtful manner then said, Perhaps you could describe your own views? Share with us your Dewa samurai heritage?

Koda remained silent for a moment, staring into the crackling bonfire, then he looked up and fixed Gompatchi with his gaze. Samurai kill people. That's what they do.

By which you mean kill those deserving of death.

Koda's expression didn't waver. People. Whoever is available.

Gompatchi returned his challenge. You're all alone here.

Fighting many opponents is no more difficult than fighting one, Koda said.

You could be overwhelmed.

I don't think so.

You don't think so…

The many will wish to co-ordinate themselves because each man hopes to survive. The man alone has the advantage. And his strategy unremarkable.

You are threatening us?

No.

But you feel you could defeat us?

Yes.

Gompatchi sat pondering this for a moment. I don't believe you could do it, he said finally.

One of the gamblers sitting near the communal wine pot had a matchlock pistol shoved in his sash in the manner of the southern barbarians. Start with him, Koda said. Slash him across the eyes. You'll hear his cries, see his blood, smell his fear. It will change you. You may spread yourselves apart more widely than you should. I'll cut down the men in the middle. If you close in for support, I'll swing around from the outside and you'll impede each other's sword space. He smiled. Or perhaps I'd start it another way entirely.

But you'd start it?

We're just talking, Koda said.

What about this? The samurai with the matchlock jerked it out. It'll shoot a hole right through you!

Koda ignored him. Once you begin, you do it all. Any weeper you take pity on will never forgive you the humiliation of it. You'll be required to confront him eventually. Better to do it now. If a man has brothers, kill them too. If you kill the husband, kill the wife. If you kill the parents, kill the children. Do not insult them by allowing them to survive. Koda looked at the men sitting around him in the flickering firelight, all of them silenced by his snakelike certainty. Then he returned his attention to Earless Gompatchi. What you said is true. No samurai should ever be imprisoned. Cut him down or let him go.

Gompatchi said nothing, but the dour Ishida samurai rinsed his wine cup then poured it full and held it out to Koda.

I don't drink wine, Koda said.

For the warmth then...

Warm yourself.

Ishida held the full cup, unsure what to do with it. I guess you have been on your own too long, he said. I guess you got out of the habit of being with other people.

THEY WERE GONE BY THE time he got back there, the floor boards stripped out and burned, all the fixtures burned for the heat that could be found in them. Even the little tray table had been thrown onto the fire, and the tatami mat had been hacked apart and burned, leaving dense wads of powdery ash in places, some of which still bore a few charred shreds of the binding brocade.

Koda searched through the outer edges of the berm-road hamlet until he found a freshly trampled path made by a party of men heading out into the moorlands. The day was cold and overcast but no snow fell; and he caught up with them at a newly-built mortuary shelter where they had paused to rest. The land there had been set aside for the city's future dead, and a few clan tombs stood erected already on the snow-filled plain, isolated and forlorn. The foundations for a bell tower occupied the edge of the new cemetery grounds, and the space for what would eventually be a grand funerary temple had been cleared and smoothed near a grove of leafless trees.

Koda watched the morose Ishida samurai as he came out to intercept him. I thought you didn't want to be with us.

He told him he just couldn't sleep there.

I guess you have refined tastes.

I don't like other people around me when I'm sleeping.

Ishida said most people thought being together was safer.

I guess that means I'm not like you.

Ishida looked off at the snow-covered hills beyond the moorlands. Then why are you following us?

The gamblers had built a fire at the front edge of the mortuary shelter and distributed the rations for their midday meal. They had a cask of rice wine that they heated in an iron pot then dipped out with a ladle, and they had wine cups fashioned out of sections of green bamboo.

Koda picked at the rations he'd been given, moving bits around in a simulation of eating.

Gompatchi studied him then held out his makeshift wine cup to be filled again. So what happened to your basket hat?

I decided I didn't like it.

You didn't like it. So then are we to assume you're no longer living the life of an Emptiness Monk?

Koda looked at him for a moment then said, I guess not.

And were you ever? said the matchlock owner.

They finished their meal and poured the rest of the wine into their big pot then broke apart the wine cask and began feeding bits of it into the fire, the inner surfaces of the wooden slats hissing and steaming as they charred. A couple of the gamblers went outside to piss, choosing to do so behind one of the newly erected family tombs.

I bet pissing in front of people is another thing he won't do, said the matchlock owner.

A rat-faced gambler said he thought pissing on tombs was wrong.

I guess the dead won't mind.

The rat-faced gambler said he thought they would mind. It was his understanding that the ghosts which collected near new tombs were of a particularly virulent type due to the absence of the moderating effect of the company of the older dead.

That's not it, said the senior mat sweeper. They're just ashamed.

Ashamed? The pistol owner dipped out another large cup of wine for himself. What a stupid idea.

Ashamed of being dead, said the mat sweeper. When someone dead looks at you, what they want is not to be rejected. It was the mat sweeper's responsibility to manage the flow of a game, and the other gamblers respected him and paid attention to his opinions.

I guess I never heard anything like that, said the rat-faced gambler, and Earless Gompatchi said it was news to him too.

They know you're disgusted by them, said the senior mat sweeper. And they are too. How could they not be? What they want is not to be blamed for it.

Blamed for being dead? said the man with the pistol. He glanced at Koda. You ever hear of anything like that?

No.

As if it's their fault they got that way? And that's why they feel ashamed? You don't see how stupid that is?

No one said anything then Koda said, It's never anyone's fault.

I guess that's what I just said, said the pistol owner. I guess we agree.

Every man's death holds him, Koda said. Like a thing in a hand. And every year you go past your death-day without knowing how special it is. Of course you can't know. But if you could, would you? What would it be like to know the day of your death but not the year?

Or know the year but not the day? said the rat-faced gambler.

That's it too, said Gompatchi. But which would you choose?

The gamblers looked at each other, afternoon drinkers pondering thoughts of sufficient novelty and merit as to require careful consideration.

I'll tell you the one I wouldn't choose would be the day of it, Earless Gompatchi said.

Because you'd worry as it came closer, said the mat sweeper. But think how free you'd feel on all the other days. You could do anything, fight anybody.

I'll drink to that, said the pistol man sarcastically, and he drained his cup then refilled it.

But what a thing to know, said the rat-faced gambler, also dipping out more wine.

But knowing your death-year, too, said the mat sweeper although they agreed that knowing the year of it would be less binding.

Unless of course you keep hanging on and hanging on, said Gompatchi, and everybody else is paying off their debts and cleaning house and getting ready for the end-of-year celebrations...

The rat-faced gambler laughed. And you're just sitting there all alone. Hoping maybe death forgot.

How could you do that? said the pistol man, his face pink with wine, and his grin loose and easy. That's a stupid hope.

You'd still hope it.

Still a stupid idea, he said, drinking.

Or like death got the year wrong, the senior mat sweeper said, a clerical error not caught in time; and they smiled at that idea and shoved the last of the cask slats onto their scrappy bonfire.

The man with the matchlock emptied his cup then dipped it full again, slopping wine over the edge. He held it out to Koda. Fellowship of the gang.

I don't drink.

Just one.

Koda said nothing.

One for you, said the pistol man, still pushing it towards him. Cheer you up.

Koda took the makeshift wine cup and held it then gave it back. Like I said.

You won't sleep where we sleep. You won't piss how we piss. And now you won't even *taste* our wine?

Koda watched him but said nothing.

He said before he doesn't like drinking, said Earless Gompatchi. All the more for you.

The pistol man held his cup as if trying to decide. Then he tilted it slightly and let a loose dribble splatter Koda's feet. Sorry.

By twilight they had reached a town large enough to sustain them. The gamblers set up a game in the local inn while the bullies and knife boys kept themselves in an annex, ready to intervene should their skills be required.

Earless Gompatchi and Ishida brought Koda to the game site. You need to understand how to read the room, Gompatchi said. Separate the outside from the inside.

Koda said nothing, but he was listening.

There are occasions when unscrupulous types will try to rob us. They'll usually have one or two in the game. You need to understand how it should be so you can recognise when it's going wrong.

They ran that game until just before dawn then slept a few hours and started the next one in mid-afternoon. Most of the fighters and knife boys sat around the fire pit in the back, distracting themselves with a pot of cloudy rice wine that they warmed over the fire in the hopes of masking the sourness of it. Earless Gompatchi had continued to instruct Koda in the art of the way of the flower-cards, with Ishida adding comments occasionally. They ordered another pot of the cloudy wine and platters of titbits to go with it, and Koda slung his too-long sword across his back and went outside.

The sun hung low in winter mist above the western hills, spreading a reddish tinge throughout the cloud-wash there while the snow-covered slopes darkened with arriving shadows. Koda crossed through the snow field then stopped and stood gazing at the streaks of red behind the blackness of the far hills, the pale aquamarine of the upper sky lovely, the water star low on the horizon. He stood looking at it for a long time, the beauty at the end of a winter day, the world waiting as the light sank away.

A shooting contest. The matchlock owner had come

out behind him. He drove a patched ball into the firing chamber with his ramrod then primed the pan. The trunk of that dead pine down there.

I don't like guns.

I didn't ask what you liked.

The other fighters had followed him outside, and Earless Gompatchi came out too. Put it away, he said.

The matchlock owner blew on the punk cord until it glowed then used both thumbs to ease the serpentine forward to half-cock. He chose an exaggerated firing stance with his arm extended, pointing the pistol in the direction of the target. You have your skills and I have mine. Then he turned slowly as if he'd anticipated a response he wasn't hearing, bringing his arm around too, not quite aiming at Koda but showing him what that might be like. You look a little worried now, he said, enjoying himself, twisting his wrist this way and that in a demonstration of bravado that was both a threat and the parody of one.

Then he sat down hard. His arm lay on the ground beside him still gripping the pistol. He looked up at Koda amazed, blood flooding out of the stump where his arm had been. Then his face blanked white and his eyelids fluttered, and he lay back on the icy surface of trampled snow and sighed. He blinked his eyes as if to clear them from some irritation then sighed again and stopped blinking them.

Koda reached down and plucked up the hem of the dying man's robe. He cleaned the edge of his too-long sword with it.

The others all stood there looking at him.

I don't like guns, Koda said.

Earless Gompatchi turned away, and the others followed him back inside, but Ishida stayed with him. That shouldn't have happened like that, he said.

Koda returned his too-long sword over his shoulder into its scabbard, the sweep of it sliding home like the sound of a nightjar's cry. But it did.

The Plantain

芭 蕉 樹

The silk merchant slid open the side panel on his palanquin. Has it come yet?

Ohasu nodded, shivering from the cold, and she fell in at the rear of the file of attendants as the silk merchant was carried up the snow-covered hill to the gate.

Kichiji had purchased this cottage for Old Master Bashō, judging it large enough for linked poetry sessions but not so large as to jeopardise the old man's reputation for austerity; and he had outfitted it with all the cushions and quilts and crockery and trays required for domestic life.

The silk merchant was a large and fleshy man, much troubled by chilblains in winter; and he waited for his chock-bearer to prepare an easy place for him to dismount.

So there it is, Kichiji said; and Ohasu nodded, teeth chattering, her single gaudy robe and satin cloak providing little protection against the icy day.

I said, there it is.

Yes! said Ohasu quickly. That is indeed it.

A large plantain rested on a bullock dray. Its fronds were bundled up and tied with rice-straw ropes, and its root-ball was wound around and around with another rope and decorated with a few celebratory sprigs of fern fronds and strips of white blessing paper cunningly folded. The bullock stood with his head down, his breath issuing from wet black nostrils in vapourous bursts that seemed incongruous for such a massive and torpid beast.

It seems like a good one, said Ohasu, but the silk merchant made no reply.

The gardeners had scraped away the snow just inside the front gate and built a bonfire to cover an area slightly wider than they would need. The head gardener told the silk merchant that although his request was peculiar, it did provide an opportunity to instruct apprentices in the method of setting large plants in winter. You can tell them in words. But they are useless until they've done it with their own hands.

Kichiji smiled benignly but said nothing.

The gardeners had a reed-mat to sit on, but the afternoon was too cold so they stood beside the fire flapping their arms and stomping their feet as they waited for the frozen earth to loosen.

Is the old man not here?

He's still inside, said Ohasu. She was a scrawny little pleasure provider prone to moments of melancholy and so not sought after by the spendthrifts and gallants and easy-way boys whose lurid exploits set the pace in the pleasure quarters of Yoshiwara. Ohasu was, however, clever with words, and this made her a suitable choice for the less demanding social requirements of *haikai* poets. He asked me to watch for you, she said, and stuffed her hands more deeply into her sleeves.

The gardeners had brought iron thrust-bars for cracking open the frozen soil, and a pair of heavy adzes with flat steel blades. They studied the low white sky like discomfort connoisseurs and speculated on how long the snow would hold off. The gardeners had a cask of liquid manure mixed with leaf mould. Beside it was a smaller cask of rice wine, and much of the humour of their banter involved variations on the dismay they would feel should one container be mistaken for the other.

Old Master Bashō spotted the silk merchant and came outside. He was draped with an additional padded robe and wore a scholar's cap on his bald skull. It's good of you to come, said the old poet. Kichiji had also funded the recent publication of a compendium of the group's linked poetry that included one of his own modest efforts, albeit in a form heavily rewritten by the Old Master. And on such a frigid day. The little pleasure provider stood between the two men, looking from one to the other, trembling in confirmation of the cold.

The gardeners had put together a smaller fire near the ground mat and arranged rocks beside it to support their wine kettle. It takes the chill off, said the head gardener. His apprentices prepared the wine and warmed the drinking cups too. Working in the cold season requires preparations.

Across the river, Edo lay blanketed under the fresh snowfall, pale umbilicals of smoke from ten thousand kitchen fires rising straight up into the white sky that lowered over the city like an immense medusa; and in the far distance glowed the massive cone of Mount

Fuji, a slender banner of cloud trailing away from the peak.

They poured out the wine when it was ready, and the Old Master and Kichiji each accepted a cup.

With all respect, said the head gardener, I was surprised to hear that such a plant as this had been requested. You would have been better off with a plum there or a peach. The climate's too cold for a plantain. It won't fruit. And the wind off the river will tear the leaves.

Our teacher had a plantain near the gate of his previous cottage, said Kichiji. It is how our linked poetry group is known.

That may be so. The head gardener sipped at his wine, pleased with the opportunity to display his expertise. Nevertheless, you'll get no shade, the wood's useless, and the flowers are just little green knots. No one will even notice them.

Probably the poets will, said Ohasu.

But couldn't you just as well be known as the peach tree group? That way you'd get a good name plus fruit in summer.

Once the fire had died away, the gardeners began cracking down through the soil, prying up frozen clods and breaking them apart until they had reached below the frost line and could dig more freely. They allowed ash from the fire to mix in with the loose dirt at the bottom of the hole then poured in a layer of the compost mixture.

Don't put the wine in! one cautioned, and the others all laughed heartily.

The first snowfall, what happiness to be in my own house.

KICHIJI JOINED OLD MASTER Bashō beside his brazier. Ohasu placed a water basin on the iron trivet and heated a flask of rice wine. There were titbits in a stacking-box in the pantry, and she arranged the best ones nicely on a platter. She had thought they might attempt a three-poet winter sequence together and had sat up the night before preparing a few ideas of her own, but neither man mentioned such an undertaking and she couldn't suggest it herself.

The silk merchant and the old poet talked of various things, the warmth and the wine creating a pleasant mood; and in a burst of enthusiasm that seemed spontaneous but wasn't, the silk merchant recommended that the Old Master keep Ohasu permanently.

The Old Master's cheeks were pink and his small eyes were closed to slits. She has her own life in the pleasure quarters.

No kind of life at all, said Kichiji. She would be more useful here. He finished his cup and Ohasu poured it full for him then turned with the flask to wait for the Old Master to finish his.

This cottage is very small.

She is small herself, declared Kichiji cheerfully. Just look at her.

Neither man did.

That two-mat room off the scullery could be cleaned out. Her bedding would fit in the cubby there, and her robes could be hung from hooks embedded in the wall.

Places could be found for her decorations and cosmetics and whatever other little things she has. We worry that you're too much on your own.

The old *haikai* poet held up his cup to be refilled. The loneliness of solitude seemed less of a burden to him than did the loneliness he felt when in the company of others; and while he recognized his withdrawal as a form of selfishness, he saw no remedy for it. What he wanted was to look at the facts of the world steadily enough to see them as they really are. But he also wanted to record what he found, and the words he used entangled him in distortions so that these attempts at preservation destroyed the things sought.

The teahouse that holds her contract is in my debt, the silk merchant continued. Reaching an agreement would be a simple matter.

Old Master Bashō agreed to consider taking possession of Ohasu; and after the silk merchant and the little peony girl had finally departed, he went outside again to view his new acquisition.

The plantain's long fronds shone gray-green in the gathering twilight. Snow crystals had collected already in central rosette of the plant; and as he stood with it, bits of ice arrived skittering down the broad fleshy leaves with a sound like mice scampering across a dry ceiling. The sour tang of liquid manure rising coldly to his nostrils was also part of it for him, of what he wished from it; and the old poet waited with the plant then walked out through his brushwood gate and stood looking down the empty road. What would remain after he died? A few books, a few paintings, a collection of words arranged and rearranged, a hoard of imitators squabbling over continuity, and one or two other followers who would struggle to trace out those parts of him which twisted similarly within themselves and who would sooner or later conclude that he too had been a fraud.

But then he'd always known that, and he decided he would wait for a couple of days before refusing the silk merchant's offer.

On an old gilt screen, the image of an ancient pine: winter seclusion.

OHASU SPENT THAT NIGHT with a visitor who had not requested her. He was a rice broker from Sakai City come to Edo to track down his son, who had absconded after looting the family strongbox. The rice broker did not want entertainment. But he also didn't want to be alone, and he purchased a night at the House of the Lesser Tada on the understanding it would be shared but without stipulating with whom.

Ohasu poured his wine and served his food and ate and drank with him. The rice broker didn't want to talk about his son's betrayal, and he didn't want to talk about anything else; but he also didn't want to just sit there and brood so Ohasu chatted away, avoiding the usual pleasure-quarters gossip about heroic tales of concupiscent audacity for fear that his son's motives might be linked to such adventures; and as the rice broker showed no interest in finger games or smutty tunes or comic dances, she soon exhausted familiar topics and blurted out that he might be her last visitor.

So you would leave this life willingly? And did you also find it easy to abandon your parents' home and come here?

She said she might have an opportunity to become the housekeeper for a famous *haikai* poet. It was a world of words that she had long wished to –

Not what I asked, declared the rice broker harshly.

I did leave my home. And it was not easy for me. Ohasu told him she had been lonely as a child because her family was even poorer than the others in their village, and it was poverty that had resulted in her being sold to the pleasure quarters. She was small for her age, and she had been mocked in her village because of her fondness for insects. Beetles, butterflies, crickets, any little being that crawled or fluttered had pleased her. Even the giant stag beetles village boys collected and pitted against each other in bug sumo bouts found favour in her eyes; and she would keep her own specimens in cages formed from bamboo twigs, bringing them out when no one else was around for the pleasure of watching as they went about their affairs.

She told him how she had loved the sound of bell crickets in autumn, how she had followed butterflies in spring and cicadas in summer, and how she had searched for winter spiders clinging to life under the frozen eaves of their poor dwelling. But what I loved best were caterpillars, the fuzzy green ones with tufts of yellow and white bristles on their backs. She told him how she used to sit near the bushes her favourites chose for their cocoons and watch them spinning the protection they created for themselves.

The rice broker drank and held his cup out to be filled.

Ohasu told him that her family was too poor to afford *hina* dolls for the girls' festival so she had made her own out of flowers and twigs and bits of moss, and set them up on a rock shelf in a forest dell. She had invited insect guests to view her dolls, selecting beetles or mantises that could be compelled to respond in an orderly manner and marching them past her display using twigs to guide them.

The rice broker from Sakai sat listening to Ohasu's chatter without comment. The wine was making him increasingly bitter, for his son's betrayal felt like the stab of a sneak assassin.

Ohasu poured his wine cup full then filled her own. It's rude of me to go on and on about myself, she said. I apologise.

The rice broker nodded then emptied his cup. Who are you to become a housekeeper for a poet? he demanded; and when Ohasu started to explain her hopes again, he leaned forward and slapped her sharply across the face, not so hard as to leave a mark but hard enough to cause pain. Such selfishness, he muttered, and held out his wine cup to be refilled.

Solitary Rambler on the Withered Moor

枯 野 一 人

It's not right.

It's the way it is.

But it needs to cut through. She chopped the air with the blade of her hand. End the gloomy mood.

But Hasegawa *liked* his idea – the melancholy image of a lost sandal sunk to the bottom of a winter pond – and he wanted to keep it.

Try it my way and see, said Little Ohasu.

A porcelain pot brazier was sufficient to heat her small room. She draped her two gaudy robes over a rack fitted against the back wall, one salmon and gold silk, the other an icy green with sprays of reeds in silver appliqué. Her bedding fitted into a storage space beside her display alcove. She had floor cushions and a small tray table and a mirror stand with the mirror safely covered. Old Master Bashō had drawn an ink sketch of a kettle on a trivet for her, a few wisps of steam rising up faintly through a haiku praising the pleasures of winter interiors. She'd hung it in her alcove and arranged a few winter chrysanthemums for it in an old ginger jar.

So, then, 'A summer shower, with the raindrops visible only when –'

No. 'An *evening* shower, with the...'

Right. '...with the raindrops visible only when...'

'Lightning flashes.'

Right. 'Lightning flashes.' Then ... 'blue herons wading alone under ...' yellow kerria roses, was it?

'At the water's edge, blue herons wading each alone: yellow kerria roses.'

Hasegawa thought about it. You're right. He inked his brush and wrote her stanza on their shared sheet. But I'll also keep mine, he said, jotting it down on a scrap of paper. I may want to use it later.

You'll almost certainly *try* to, Ohasu said.

He looked at her. You're mocking me.

I would *never* do that! she cried, laughing. How could I?

The rogue samurai Hasegawa Torakage stayed away when she had visitors, and she understood that he accepted the requirements of her life in the floating world much in the way he reconciled himself to his own disreputable occupation. Ohasu's skill as a *haikai* poet meant she attracted pleasure seekers who often wished to while away an evening by comparing seashells, playing the poem-card game, or listening to lugubrious old ballads about martial exploits long since forgotten.

Instead of 'blue herons', it could be 'white egrets'.

'Blue herons' is better.

He thought about it. All right.

They matched each other stanza for stanza; and while Hasegawa's reading of old poetry books resulted in links that reverberated with the muted echoes of ancient temple bells, Ohasu was the one who found a surprising new music in the patterns that emerged. Things never before attempted were done for the first time. Hasegawa sorted through old locutions like a pauper counting rice grains with a needle while Ohasu attached silk ribbons to flying birds. Trusted histories sprouted with improbable curiosities. Angels in feathered cloaks descended through misty moonlight to encounter toads croaking under cedar tubs; textures shimmered, colours danced and sang. And although Hasegawa's samurai heritage trapped him in uncertainty – prerogatives had been curtailed yet obligations remained – nothing was expected of a girl like Ohasu, and she flung open doors for him to peer into if not enter, even when they were lying naked together under her quilts. But one cold winter twilight as they sat in her window watching the first flakes of a fresh snowfall arriving with the dusk, she started to ask why he seemed so remote but then didn't because she guessed what he would tell her and wasn't willing to ruin the day by hearing it said again yet also found in her own reluctance a gap opening between them and so did ask it and was told.

Hasegawa was ashamed of what he had become. His mother had died with his father and brothers, and he had never been able to forgive her for it. Her choice had become the absence around which he had arranged himself, peering down into it now and again then pulling away. He had been required to accept her death and had failed to do so. It was rimless, a void with no edges; and just as she had become unavailable, her death also had been denied him. He had listened to what was said about it ever since he was a small boy and understood the words but not what they meant. She was a samurai wife, a daughter of the Land of Dewa, and her submission to necessity was the flower of her life. But what he had wanted as a boy, what he wanted still, was access to whatever lay beneath those easy explanations.

I haven't asked anything of you, Ohasu said.

No. Not directly.

How then?

He thought that the shame of his yearning for his mother to have chosen to live for him would be impossible for a non-samurai to grasp. It's not something to talk about, Hasegawa said.

But why not?

The night before she died, his mother had put him to bed in a separate room. A child of six, he had guessed that something was wrong but had not known how to ask about it. The following morning, awakened by unfamiliar sounds, he had run outside to find mounted warriors waiting at the gate of the compound, the crests on their sleeves showing them to be Tokugawa retainers. Five confirmation-head caskets of pale wood were on the veranda corridor already sealed, and his grandfather was washing blood off his fingers.

Because it's mine, Hasegawa said. And I can't share it.

Yours...

Hasegawa's mother and father and three brothers had each been assisted by his grandfather in order to preserve the honour of the family, and his grandfather would also have been the one to lower each head carefully into its cylindrical casket and pour in the rice wine preservative then fit on the lid, tapping it down properly in preparation for the trip to Edo.

Yours? Ohasu jerked one of her gaudy robes off the rack and wrapped herself in it. Is this why? Her obi sashes were rolled neatly and stacked in the corner. She released them across the tatami floor mats one by one, the lustrous brocades of gold and silver and pink and bronze overlapping each other in the muted light from the white paper lantern. Is what I am making you what you are? Her hair ornaments and other decorations were kept in a cedar box. She dumped everything out in a heap. Are these things pinching you?

No.

Should I stop wearing them? I can't, of course. But do you want me to?

Hasegawa looked at his hands. I don't have any right to ask anything of you...

But he still did it. You're doing it now! Clutching the loss of his samurai dreams for the pleasure of feeling sorry for himself.

It's not like that...

But it was.

What choice do I have?

She didn't know. It was too much for her to take in. But she sat with the additional gaudy robe still draped over her narrow shoulders, trying to work her way back up to a solution or at least an alternative explanation, once again negotiating the gap between what she wanted and what she could have.

The charcoal banked; but on the wall, the guest's shadow.

THINGS THEY USED TO find easy to say now went un-said. Ohasu accepted evening engagements she might previously have declined; and Hasegawa, left on his own, would hang around the edges of public rooms or wander aimlessly through winter lanes.

Yet when Ohasu received a gift of fine writing pa-per, she shared it with him; and when a client awarded her with a wonderful Chinese ink stick, she broke it in half. On some afternoons, they were as they had been; and skeins of words were twisted into cable-strands that bound together a shimmering world of images. Violets bloomed under hedges; a hawk smoothed its feathers in the steady rain; fat puppies chewed on melon rinds; hoarfrost crusted the leaves of a cotoneas-ter. But Hasegawa knew Ohasu was waiting for some-thing he could not give her, and she knew he knew it.

They decided to spend a whole day making a hun-dred-stanza sequence in imitation of the medieval three-poet style. They brought in extra fuel as well as a crock of wine, plenty of tea, and boxes of rice cakes topped with pressed fish. They hung a taboo tag on the closed door, suspecting that someone would probably add a comic desecration to it, for the other peony girls preferred the livelier world of music and dancing, fash-ion and the new kabuki theatre.

Their intention was to finish the sequence before twilight, and they would not indulge in wine or food until the entire hundred stanzas were completed, or at least not excessively. Each would compose a stanza alone then they would create the third-poet stanzas together and sign these, 'The Solitary Rambler on the Withered Moor,' a name they judged suitably exotic. They had driven the sequence forward despite occasional quarrels – the shared stanza usually the source of disagreement – until Ohasu suggested, 'The cold season: in the weak winter sunlight, pickled radish slices in a Holland-style dish,' an image that Hasegawa thought too eccentric for a formal sequence.

But it's a clear glass dish, you see, and so cool in its transparency...

But from Holland? How can you include such a bizarre place?

But that's the idea! She smiled at him. But of course if it's a problem for you because it's never been used before...

I don't just get things from what I've read!

She smiled mischievously. Of course you don't.

And the image is cool, not cold, said Hasegawa stubbornly, not 'cold-season' cold. And how do you even know about such things?

Ohasu removed the pot of winter chrysanthemums on her alcove display shelf then pried up one of the shelf-boards and retrieved a hidden parcel. On the lid of a wooden box were words written in the butter-eaters' alphabet, ugly awkward glyphs that Hasegawa thought looked like the tracks of chickens; and inside the box was a small, clear glass bowl. She lifted it out. Hollanders also have cups made of glass that they use to drink grape wine, said Ohasu. Grape wine is red.

Red?

Like blood! She shuddered at the grotesque idea.

He took it from her. You can't have seen butter eaters do such things?

No. How could I? But it would be like drinking blood out of a piece of ice.

Hasegawa handed the bowl back to her. Where did you get it?

From one of my friends. Ohasu held the little glass bowl in both hands. You say you have to keep what's yours. Let me keep what's mine.

I wish you had other things.

You mean you wish I was different.

Hasegawa watched as Ohasu replaced the little glass bowl in its box. I wish we both were, he said.

Sometimes Hasegawa would be in her room when Ohasu returned from the afternoon bath. He would sit in the corner with a book or sheaf of poems open before him, reading out stanzas he liked while Ohasu readied herself for the evening. Oyuki or one of the other peony girls came in occasionally, and they would chat about what awaited them, discussing strategies and contingencies. Much that seemed spontaneous was made to seem that way. Nape lines were adjusted, bodices managed. Despite the chill of winter, they never wore more than a single gaudy-robe over a red silk underskirt that showed when the skirt flap folded open. They wound on their wide obi sashes in a manner that would suit an evening's requirements so that a girl who on one occasion might present herself as a maiden too shy to speak would on the next be proclaimed the possessor of concupiscent urges of such fervour and audacity that once the wine began flowing, great care must be taken, for there was no way to predict what kind of mischief might occur to her.

Hasegawa in his corner listened to their appraisals of the guests they would be serving. Osome, a new girl in her first season, was often unsure; and Oyuki and Ohasu would advise her on how to control the flow of an evening, when to yield and when to resist. Sometimes guests became too lively and their bad behaviour had to be tolerated. Other times they could be distracted by guessing games or improvised contests. If one girl was being abused, then the others should try to charm her abuser. Lure tickle-teasers into hallways. Encourage drunks to sing. Feed bullies to the point of torpor. But if a man becomes too rowdy or behaves in an intolerable manner, then tell me, Ohasu said, and I'll tell Hasegawa; and he will speak with the offending person and settle matters.

The new girl had glanced at the rogue samurai in the corner. But what if he can't?

He usually can.

But if he fails?

Then we'll light the building on fire, Oyuki declared. And with loud cries throw ourselves into the flames!

Osome had goggled at her credulously.

Or just run away, said Ohasu.

Or put up with it, Oyuki added; and they had all three looked at Hasegawa: *Or?*

There were times when Hasegawa detected within their banter an anticipation of pleasures to come. He held what he was reading without seeing the words. Some merchants were considered connoisseurs, and sometimes bureaucrats proved to be open to novel ideas. A young samurai was mocked as a rural buffoon: dung stained his sandals; his robes were not stylish; and when he spoke, it sounded like rocks rolling in a brook. But mention of his prowess with the slippery ways of love elicited knowing smiles and sly glances.

Osome wondered what if *he* created problems? Could Hasegawa solve them?

What he creates are not problems, said Oyuki; and she laughed when Ohasu cried, And how would *you* know?

Hasegawa was moving words around in his cubby late one night, hoping to hit upon fortuitous combinations, when Ohasu lurched inside, reeking with wine and tobacco smoke. I won't tell you what I did. She held out her arms for him to unwind her obi sash.

What did you do?

I won't tell you.

He hung her gaudy robe and scarlet underskirt on wall hooks then tucked her in his quilts. You don't have to, he said.

I know.

He lay down beside her but was unable to sleep so he got up and lit a small stand lamp then stirred up the coals in his brazier and added a few chunks of charcoal. He sat sit hunched beside the growing warmth, developing variations on stanzas he liked and alternating his voice with a woman's voice that sometimes seemed like Ohasu to him and sometimes like what he thought he

remembered of his mother. He connected them together in short sequences of three or four pairs, not
signing any of them because he was unable to devise a
satisfactory pseudonym for the female stanzas. He detected patterns in places he hadn't seen them before,
fitted in new links where needed to create transitions
until he had a thirty-six stanza sequence that held together from beginning to end, the pulse running
through it expanding and contracting with the consistency of the changes from female to male, the surface
flickering with transformation.

It had begun snowing again. He slid open the window to look out on the empty garden behind the assignations tea house, an extra winter robe draped over his
head as he sat in the cold, reciting to himself portions of
the sequence he had just made. He looked back at
Ohasu buried under his quilts then returned his attention to the fat wet flakes falling, the descending net of
whiteness and the space it occupied creating a sense of
distance that also seemed like an immediacy.

Hasegawa awoke just at dawn. He turned up glowing coals banked in white ash, adding fresh charcoal
and fanning it into flames. Once the low fire in his brazier seemed secure, he began to go back through what
he'd written the night before, following each phrase as
it flowed down into the next. What are you reading?
Ohasu settled beside him, wrapped in the sleeping
quilt. She leaned forward, peering down at the open
scroll. That's mine, she said, that stanza. Except not
quite like that.

I thought it needed to be ... stronger.

Stronger? She read down through the sequence. That's mine too, she said. And that one looks familiar, part of it, but not exactly...

It's how I thought you would have done it. My version of your style...

Your version of me...

I didn't say that.

No. You haven't been able to. But if you could...

She picked up the writing brush then stroked in a variation on one of her stanzas. That's more mine. More my version of me. She let the next one stay as it was then started to read the one following it and stopped. I didn't write that.

No.

Who is she?

If my mother had written something, it might have been like that.

Your mother? Ohasu read through a couple more stanzas then set the scroll aside softly and looked at him, her eyes filling with doubt. Is your version of her better than hers was too?

It's only a sequence, only words.

Ohasu continued to regard him uncertainly.

You always say how you need balance, Hasegawa said, rushing ahead with it. So I thought playing a male voice against a female voice would do it. As if it's really made by two people. That's all. A simple thing.

By three people. And hardly simple. Ohasu scanned down through the scroll again like a person looking for the name of a loved one on a list of victims. She took up the brush again and blotted out the alterations she had made. You should just keep your version of me as it is, she said.

Hasegawa's duties meant he was often gone from the pleasure quarters as he pursued samurai who had failed to honour their debts. Sometimes he recovered the full amount owed and sometimes he accepted a partial payment. There were times, too, when he found his quarry but reported back to the tea house master that he couldn't find him. Alone in his small room with his books and his inkstone, he occupied himself with the arranging of words and tried to ignore the laughter and singing in the teahouse. Evening distributions occasionally resulted in squabbles he was obliged to resolve, and he sat up listening to the sound of feet on the stairs and in the upstairs corridors, the men's tread heavier, the awkward thumps of drunks stumbling, the gasps of laughter at misunderstandings or provocations that had found a larger audience than intended.

Sometimes Ohasu slept in his room and sometimes she whispered he should sneak upstairs to hers and sometimes neither happened. One night the figure who crawled in beside him was Oyuki. She slithered out of her robes then slipped into his quilts, telling him she had escaped because she knew he was impatient, as if he were a client she was favouring. She reeked of wine fumes and laughed at her own boldness then told him she had met her dream-lover at last and could not restrain herself for the excitement of the idea of it.

But where's Ohasu?

Busy. Oyuki snuggled in beside him, resting the flesh of one breast against his arm. He's the son of a rich merchant and so stylish! His robe is appropriate for a townsman, as is his obi sash; but both are lined with raw silk said to come from the land of elephants. What audacity! Who ever heard of such a thing? Oyuki's hand had drifted down his belly and arrived on his penis. A pale apricot inside his sleeves and the inside of his sash is like the colour of pomegranate seeds and as luscious! And he knows all about the new rough-style acting that is becoming popular in Edo, and poetry too although he says only the opening stanzas are worth writing. She began stroking him up erect until he stopped her. What?

Just don't.

Why not?

The door was slapped open and Ohasu lurched inside, her obi sash unwinding behind her in a twist of brocade. Osome's like a demon granny! she cried and pulled loose her obi then piled it in a corner and dumped her gaudy robe in a heap beside it. Hopping in and out of her cave! Ohasu picked at the knot securing her red silk underskirt. They asked me if wine always made her so giddy. She got the knot loose finally and settled in with them. And I said it was the heat of their male energy that had overwhelmed her.

Oyuki laughed. And they believed you?

Ohasu tucked in against Hasegawa. They'll sleep with knives under their pillows tonight. She leaned up on one elbow. And you! You with your promises of the myriad joys of spring! What are *you* doing in here with him anyway?

The Goat Bonze

山 羊 坊 主

Takeda Nobuo sat alone under a wild cherry that was shedding its blossoms in the misty drizzle. Cherry petals flecked his rain cape and travel hat and the hilts of his two swords, and formed a pink carpet on the edge of the mountain road. He'd build a small comfort-fire against the dreary afternoon, and smoke from it rose up through the falling blossoms and into the low white sky.

Some masterless samurai found independence profitable. They sold their services to local magnates who were embarking on small wars or perhaps contemplating a timely theft or assassination, or they charged hefty fees to protect valuable cargo being shipped from Edo to Miyako, or banded together with like-minded rascals and stole it. Takeda Nobuo wasn't like that. A morose and solitary money-fighter whose family had lost their home in the far northern fief of Akita as punishment for a slighting remark made by his grandfather, Takeda took on projects that seemed right to him, declined those he deemed dishonourable, and went hungry when his money ran out. What was left of his family had dispersed throughout the archipelago; and when they encountered each other they sat together in silence, for there was little to be said about the evil fate that had befallen them.

Takeda looked up to see a Zen bonze ambling towards him and leading a pair of piebald goats on rice-straw ropes. The bonze wore a shabby black robe patched in places, and his cowl, such as it was, seemed to serve various purposes, not all of which were salubrious. The stubble on his bald head was the same length as the stubble on his cheeks and chin, and he carried a walking staff with a few iron rings attached to the top as a jingle warning against insects that might wander into his path.

The bonze halted in front of the Akita samurai. End of the blossoming season up here, he said. If the wind doesn't do it the rain will.

Takeda nodded but said nothing.

The goats wanted the grass on the road verge opposite so the bonze moved over there with them. He looped each goat's lead rope around the hind leg of the other and knotted it with a deft yank.

The bonze said he had gone to preside at the funeral of a relative he hardly knew and had come away in possession of the man's goats. No one else had wanted them. They'd all just stood there looking at them. He said he didn't want them either, but the only other solution seemed to be to set them free or kill them and he didn't want that. He said it wasn't appropriate for a Zen bonze to own anything so he considered himself to be a guider of wayward goats. He said the word 'wayward' described them as it did most other sentient beings. If the goats were a nuisance at times there was also a certain amount of pleasure to be gained from their company. They get a little reeky, said the Zen man, particularly when wet. But then I guess I get that way too.

The bonze dropped into a squat in the middle of the road with his black monk's robe tucked up between his thighs. Of course, they might become a hindrance on begging rounds. You could be standing there all solemn and deep in somebody's doorway, and with your begging bowl held in this irresistible manner that has devised by you after careful experimentation on what sanctity looks like when its starving ... and then realise your goats were back there in the garden feeding on radish tops!

Takeda smiled at the garrulous bonze.

On the other hand, they might become a curiosity. He nodded in fairness to himself. Hard to predict how a person might feel about a goat.

I guess that's true.

The bonze remained as he was. Of course, a lot of people in this country don't even know we have goats here.

Takeda said nothing.

Probably came originally from China or Korea. He studied the Akita samurai who was morosely tending his fire then said, I just came from a funeral but you look like the one in mourning.

The goats had started moving in opposite directions. Their catch ropes tautened until each was pulling the other's back end around in a disconcerting manner, and they were soon jerking and hauling at each other until the bonze restored order.

He squatted back down again then said, I guess you don't want to talk about it.

Takeda poked at his fire then looked up at him. I killed some people.

All right.

I mean just recently. This morning.

He continued observing him. In a fight?

A fight. He thought about it. An unfair fight.

You said some people?

Five men.

And that was the unfairness? Five against one?

No, Takeda said. The unfairness was that I knew how to kill them, but they didn't know how to kill me.

I see, said the bonze, the settling mist more like low clouds than rain, the falling cherry petals adhering to the rocks and tree trunks, sticking to whatever they touched. You don't seem remorseful, he said.

I'm not.

But you aren't pleased about it either.

No.

All right. He watched his goats tearing out mouthfuls of lush grass again, loops of green slime wobbling off their chin beards. A hard situation.

The Akita samurai poked at his fire, sending up a flurry of sparks. I'd do it again. But I'm sorry I did it. He levered one burning stick up onto another. But I'd kill them again. So I guess that doesn't make much sense.

The goat bonze watched him. You hated them that much?

I thought I did.

And now you have doubts?

No. No doubts.

But you decided you didn't hate them as much as you'd thought?

I guess maybe that's it. He began shoving the un-burned ends of sticks onto the centre of his fire. I guess I think I knew that doing it wouldn't make me feel any better about things. But I did it anyway.

Because not doing it would have been worse?

Maybe that's it.

You don't sound sure.

No. I don't.

They harmed you?

They killed a woman who was in my care.

I see. So it was a serious matter then.

Yes.

But you aren't satisfied with your decision.

No. I am.

You don't seem it.

I guess not, said the samurai.

The Zen man nodded, squatting in the road, as if one place for him was as good as any other. I guess even an egg can think it's a rock. Until it meets a rock.

I guess that must be just about it, said Takeda. But he smiled again and the bonze smiled too, except then he asked why the men had killed the woman and was told that they had fucked her without permission and were afraid she would tell someone who could do something about it.

Meaning you.

Meaning me.

And this all happened this morning?

No. Last summer. I just found them this morning. He poked at the fire. They were hard to find. Because they knew I would be looking for them.

The bonze said, You cared that much for this woman?

No. I didn't know her. I was just paid to escort her to Miyako.

But still the violation of her would –

It was the violation to me, said Takeda.

I see. The bonze pulled a stick out of the fire and used it to arrange the coals on his side, moving things around in a helpful manner before tossing the stick back into the flames. You know, probably their souls are already getting ready for the hovering part. Forty-nine days of shivering with anticipation. Lined up like ants in a food file. Although probably for what they did, they won't come back very well. He studied the samurai tending his meagre fire and said, Probably you won't either.

All right.

All right. The bonze shoved his hand into the front flap of his robe and scratched himself thoughtfully. A flea, a horsefly, a wasp, something such as that might be about as good as you wrathful types can hope for. You were told the truth but you didn't hear it. Do the right things. Live the right way. Simple enough when you think about it. But even if you're only a horsefly on the next loop through, you can still be a good one.

A good one?

A horsefly has a horsefly's virtues.

I don't care much for horseflies.

Most people don't.

Probably you've never had horses in warm weather. The way they're tormented by them.

Horseflies are a horse's fate.

I'd kill every one of them if I could.

Well! Another step down the slippery road to hell.

The Akita samurai smiled at himself. But I still mean it.

You're that fond of horses?

I used to be. I guess I still am. Just that I haven't had one recently. He thought about it. I guess I don't have a lot of what I used to have.

Such as?

Things to look forward to.

All right.

People to be with, I guess. Occurrences and events. Or even just something I can say that I chose for myself...

Thread has to go where the needle went.

I understand that. He sat pondering for a long moment then said, You really believe that about their souls?

All our souls.

All our souls? That it's a return to the next turn? Each connected to the one coming?

The Zen bonze used his sleeve to wipe the moisture off his face then said, Let me ask you something. Did you ever consider the possibility that a man might obtain solace in this world of woe by taking responsibility for the well-being of goats?

I was asking about what happens after you're dead.

I know that. And I was answering it.

The Akita samurai looked back at him, unsure how to respond. He told him he did not believe there was a place for him other than the one he himself occupied at any given instant of the day. He said he awoke in the morning the same man that he'd gone to sleep as the night before. He said he'd heard a lot of things said. But among them he'd never found one he thought might be more true than the simple fact that when spring comes, grass grows by itself.

By which you mean you think you can't change.

I guess that's just about it.

The bonze watched his goats like a person confirming an hypothesis then turned back to the Akita samurai and his fire. Tell me why you killed them.

I told you.

Tell me again. Tell me better.

Takeda Nobuo stayed with his fire, adjusting it, scraping it around, the smoke rising up through the misty drizzle sinking down into it. I guess I don't know any better way of saying it.

You don't think there's an obligation?

Only to what happened. Not to describing what it was.

And so not to what it meant?

No, he said in a quiet voice. I do not believe that.

Samurai kill for pride.

Some samurai do.

But not you?

Like I said. I guess that's what I don't know.

All right. The bonze waited until he was sure Takeda had nothing more to say on the subject then got up and went to retrieve his goats. He got them untangled then stood for a moment studying the Akita samurai who seemed to him like a man who would be willing to sit by the edge of the road until the world itself shuddered to an end. Why'd you kill all of them?

Takeda poked at his fire.

You have a group like that, and one or two will be the cause of such things, and one or two will go along with it, but it seems to me there's every possibility that at least one of them didn't really deserve to die.

Which one?

Well, I don't know. No way for me to know.

Me either, Takeda said, and the bonze turned away and continued on in the direction he was taking.

Under Blossoming Boughs
花 の 下

His eyes opened to the glow of a sun not yet risen. The air was dry and cool and still, and he listened for the first stirrings of neighbours then sat up and slid open his white paper doors.

Dew coated the planks of the narrow veranda-corridor. The leaves of the potted camellia were beaded white with it, and Old Master Bashō breathed deeply in the dawn air, his thin chest rising and falling with the exaggerated effort he associated with good health. A nightingale had taken up residence in a pear tree near the communal well, but there was no sign of the bird, only the droplets of water falling ceaselessly back into the water below, regular as heartbeats.

The day's radiance had begun seeping up into misty clouds strung like peach-coloured banners above the shogun's metropolis, and with it rose the yearning to open himself to the facts of the world and to say what could be said about it.

So the sound of the water in the well, and the sound of rain on the broad, fleshy leaves of the plantain growing inside his front gate…

Or the scent of rain arriving in dust. Or the colour of rain shimmering in a hardwood forest. Or the shape of wind-driven rain striding across an empty moorlands...

Or of rain lacing the river to the sky. Or pocking late sleet still floating on the surface of an early spring pond in a bamboo grove...

Or, rather, how spring rain in a roof-top collection barrel overflows and leaks out onto the roof tiles, the stillness of it understood at the moment of its interruption ... or the murmur of rain dripping into the tub of scouring ash that was kept at the scullery door ... not what it was like but what it was...

Then he could deny himself no longer, and he turned to the splendour of the cherry tree blooming in the cooper's yard.

One branch hung over his back fence, the shell-pink clouds of blossoms glowing in the misty light with a delicate and pre-emptive beauty. He gazed at the unmoving masses of flowers fully opened at last then closed his eyes to feel the image of them more intensely; and as he did so, a temple bell sounded in the distance, the long slow reverberations of it like the voice of the earth itself, reminding him of things he'd remembered and things he'd forgotten.

Clouds of cherry blossoms: is the temple bell at Ueno? at Akasaka?

OHASU COLLECTED THE BRIGHT scarlet underskirts that had been left to air overnight on the roof-top laundry platform. A soft spring haze covered the moorlands surrounding the pleasure quarters, and she watched as a single wild cherry began to emerge from the mist like a friend come for a visit. The tree was smaller than the grand Yoshino cherry trees that shaded Middle Lane and less richly covered with blossoms. No one but her seemed even aware of it. She used to hide up here when she first arrived in the pleasure quarters, a frightened little girl with no understanding of what was expected of her; and one morning in early spring she'd noticed the first faint traces of pink on the boughs of the little tree, and found comfort in it.

Hidden in the pouch of her sleeve was a paper packet held closed with a twist of rice straw twine. Ohasu untied the fastener then folded open the little parcel to reveal two cubes of candied agar-agar, the translucent brownish-green gel dusted on top with golden honey crystals and glistening like the surface of the spring sea. One of her regular visitors had brought out a box of them for her. He was a diminished old fellow and his courting had become feeble. She tried to encourage him with silly games and smutty gossip, but sustaining the throb of love's urgency was beyond him, and he would inevitably seek shelter in a wine pot.

Ohasu selected one of the cubes of agar-agar, holding it on her tongue for the sweetness of the honey. Old Master Bashō had once declared that only if you could see into the heart of a thing could you write about it; and Ohasu had wondered how you could be certain that what you were seeing was truly the heart. She sucked on the sweet candy, pressed the yielding lump of gel against the roof of her mouth. What if inside one heart you found another? She smoothed out the silk underskirts they would wear that day and folded them neatly then popped the second candy in her mouth and went back downstairs.

Spring arrives in the faint haze that wreathes these nameless hills.

OLD MASTER BASHŌ DRIBBLED a splash of water into the well of his inkstone then began rubbing his ink stick at the upper edge, the sour-dark scent of its blackness rising into the pink glow of his neighbour's wonderful tree.

He had hoped to edit his travel journal from the previous year; but the prose sketches of places he visited and the stanzas he wrote in praise of them seemed lifeless to him now, like objects draped with cloths so that shapes remained even as the things themselves became obscured. What he wanted was to make statements about the world that deserved to exist in it; but ideas accumulated, images multiplied, and even as he sought to cut out unneeded phrases, new ones occurred to him so that no matter how much he removed, too much remained.

He sat listening to the sound of night shutters being shoved one by one into their frame-holders, and the flimsy rattle of privy doors slapped open then closed. He would be obliged to spend this day – the most precious of the season – with merchant poets composing a thirty-six stanza linked poem. His fees would pay for his life for a month. Yet that hardly seemed adequate compensation for what would be lost.

Old Master Bashō shaved his head and wore a

monk's robes. But his religion was the way of *haikai* linked poetry, and the hope of his reverence was to perfect the art of his manner. Noble houses in the Old Imperial Capital of Miyako had retained control over poetry even as they surrendered the management of their vast estates to local servants who developed skills with weapons and a willingness to use them. These samurai grew in power over the centuries, and the noble families had to accept what they could not oppose. They published anthologies that included their own poems in with those of their precursors, and arranged them in sequences stipulated by the change of the seasons or the depredations of love. The art of linked poetry grew out of this tradition. It became a haven for those who felt encumbered by the centuries of civil warfare that swept across the archipelago so that even after the country had been stabilised by the Tokugawa family, the canon of literary beauty that had been achieved in the face of martial chaos thrived, and samurai with honed blades also occupied themselves with writing brushes.

Old Master Bashō began sketching out a few *hokku* head stanzas that could be used to start the sequence they would make that day, and from far in the distance came the first tentative squawks of the fresh bean-curd vendor's horn, lonely as a heron's cry. No breeze rose; yet the branch of cherry blossoms hanging over the back fence trembled slightly, lifting itself into the arriving light and drifting to him like a boat in a dream on a river.

Recollecting various things: the blooming of cherry blossoms.

BLOOD-RED SOUL BANNERS hung in a great swollen mass under the peak of the eaves of the shrine, the older ones at the centre faded now but those on the top still bright with pain. The pleasure quarters had been relocated out beyond the edge of the city in a gesture of repudiation of licentious behaviour, and the souls of the unborn had been transported out there too. Ohasu waited as her friend Oyuki bowed and clapped her hands to call her losses to her. On this day too I ask for your forgiveness, Oyuki murmured. Ohasu herself never became pregnant. She didn't know why. She also didn't know if she should feel relief or regret but suspected that one day it would be the latter.

You who never were will never cease to be for me. Oyuki's face was shadowed by the tumourous red bundle suspended above her. None of soul banners bore a name. The unborn were like bits of foam floating anonymously as they transited to the yellow springs of hell although the supplications inked onto the newer strips were still legible. On your behalf I call on the pure promise of the lotus sutra. And also from the Jizō Bodhisattva who protects lost children and wayfarers, I request it for you.

Oyuki had been betrayed by a lover she trusted. He was the son of a rich merchant, famous in the pleasure quarters for wearing robes and obi sashes that were secretly lined with exotic raw silks from the land of elephants. The insides of his sleeves when folded back might show a pale apricot, a dark cinnabar, a rufous gold, or even the luscious gleam of ripe pomegranate seeds. Oyuki had given this 'Second Genji' whatever he asked for – her money, her love, the best of the gifts she received. He in return had pledged to redeem her contract one day and set her up in a cottage near his family home, where they could sink into love's languor during all hours and seasons. But his father had betrothed him to the only child of a soy brewing magnate from the west; and although the lovers had soaked their sleeves with weeping, in the end Oyuki had been left alone while her heart's desire had trudged off to his fate as an adopted heir, assuming his bride's name, her father's fortune, and the duties of family progenitor. Except she wasn't quite alone enough, and the abortifacient she had taken made her sick for weeks.

If the 'Second Genji' had felt oppressed by his new responsibilities, he soon discovered that solace could be obtained in the pleasure quarters of the Old Imperial Capital. Carnal novelties filled his nights and days; endurance matched invention; the moist joys of spring bloomed ten thousand ways; and tales of concupiscent glory soon reached Edo so that for Oyuki, the memory of the taste of his love on her lips became like that of bitter radish.

Oyuki finished her prayer. She clapped again to release the souls of her unborn, and the two girls continued down to the morning baths.

Under the trees, soup and fish salad too: cherry blossoms.

CHERRY PETALS FILTERED DOWN like flickering chips of pink light. Oyuki inserted the bridge and twisted the middle tuning peg of her samisen, the plucked note rising as the silk string tautened. They won't last the night, she said.

No, said Ohasu, gazing out at the spring river thudding past, the heavy flow risen up onto the grassy edge of the riverbank.

Oyuki flipped her long sleeves back out of the way and began adjusting the top peg and bottom peg, sending those tones too soaring upwards. Osome's late again, she said, and Ohasu nodded but said nothing.

Oyuki plucked out the opening bars of a popular old remorse ballad as the merchant poets began arriving. They were ruddy, well-fed men, each secure in the magnitude of his own accomplishments. Sumptuary regulations required their robes to be muted shades of beige and lavender, taupe and pale gray; but dangling from silk cords on their sash pouches were cunningly wrought ivory baubles: a grinning skull, a rat on a rice bale, a sleeping cat, a snake tied in a knot.

Servants had claimed their picnic site by surrounding it with red and white striped barrier curtains then spreading red felt ground-mats on the grass. Casks of rice wine were stored against the trunk of the cherry tree they had chosen; black lacquer stacked-boxes of seasonal delicacies were arranged in the middle of the ground mat; and the fees paid for the pleasure providers would extend into the evening and include the option of negotiating for more intimate transmissions, should the need arise.

Osome pushed her way through the barrier curtains. At last! she cried, her plump cheeks rosy. She was the youngest of the peony girls and prone to misjudgements. I couldn't find it! They said under a cherry tree on the riverbank, but there are so many here!

Osome had a flowering branch clutched like a dance wand, and Oyuki whacked her samisen as if punctuating a dramatic entry in the new-style kabuki theatre so that the girl caught her cue, cocked her hip in a saucy manner and began singing, 'Oh, come and look! What won't you see? *Rice* crackers, *salmon* crackers and …' and I forget the rest of it. She hurried over to her companions, smirking at her own foolishness, and flopped down beside them, jarring loose the elaborate brocade mass of her front-tied sash knot.

The merchant poets began settling around the edge of the red felt mat; and Ohasu went to fill the long-handled pourers, the grassy scent of the pale yellow-green wine rising to greet her. A scattering of cherry petals landed on the wine cask lid, the pale pink flecks lovely against the reddish-brown lacquer surface, and she took care not to disturb them as she replaced the lid.

Osome came over to help. She held the disassembling mass of her sash knot pressed against her midriff. Which one's the famous poet? she whispered and tucked in behind the tree to reconfigure herself, still unsure how best to manage the stiff new oversized obis that were just coming into fashion.

He's not here yet, Ohasu said.

You know him, don't you.

I used to.

I wonder if he gets paid more than the three of us, said Osome.

I wonder…

Bats too come out into this floating world of birds and flowers.

PETAL FALL CONTINUED STEADILY throughout the afternoon, and every tree on the riverbank was surrounded with celebrants so that latecomers hurried along hoping for an open space somewhere farther upstream.

You don't need to control supply to secure the hemp rope market, a provisioner to the shogunate explained. But you do need to control distribution. He held out his cup and Ohasu poured for him. Manage your carters, the provisioner said, watching Oyuki as she worked out the complexities of a new song. And your dockers, too. Keep them sweet.

'What won't you see…' Oyuki picked tentatively at the opening phrases of the new dance song, mistiming the tricky up-pluck syncopation. 'Lips and … and tongue…' Not right, she tried it again. 'A husband's lies and a something something and lips and … lips and … tongue…' I just can't get that part!

You're too tentative, said Ohasu, starting around with the wine pourers again. Just jump at it.

Jump at it?

You have to make it bigger. Up quick then down hard.

Are you talking about me? A cotton merchant called out, his face flushed already with wine.

Or you could cheat and finger-pluck it with your left hand, said Osome; but Ohasu said, No, the next down-stroke still has to be timed properly. Up big then down. She chopped the beat with her free hand, the wrist loose as if wielding a plectrum; and the cotton merchant tried again: So, it's a thing that goes up and gets hard then comes back down again? he said, grinning salaciously. Whatever could it be?

Oyuki plucked out the first notes of a popular ballad in reply and sang, 'Some men yearn to find a shy beauty waiting under the blossoms...' Then she loosened her centre string, and the tone wilted in a comic deflation as she sang, 'And some to find hidden-flesh pink and slimy as the gill slits of a sea bass...'

What! cried Osome, and Ohasu laughed too. That's smutty!

You're too fast for me, said the cotton merchant, glancing around for allies; and the provisioner said, Girls swollen with the juices of spring.

Osome broke off the tip end of her blossoming branch. She plopped down beside the cotton merchant, knocking her sash knot loose again so that it erupted in a surge of bundled brocade that spilled down over his sedate brown sleeves like a sack of dropped weasels, should the weasels have been dyed to voluptuous shades of plum, pearl, salmon and cerise. 'Oh, come and look, what won't you see!' Osome inserted the spray of pink flowers in his topknot. Who can be moderate under the blossoms? She twisted sideways and leaned against the cotton merchant as she began reconfiguring her sash knot again, emitting little grunts of consternation at the effort required.

'Orange and *pink* on the…' no, it's 'orange *and* pink on the … this *and* this!' Oyuki hit the up-twang perfectly.

That's the way of it, said Ohasu, back at the tree trunk again, refilling the wine pourers.

Oyuki retuned her samisen to a ballad mode then began plucking out the lugubrious opening bars of *Green Willows Pink Blossoms,* holding each note cluster solemnly before sliding on to the next one.

'Spring rain sad in the dripping green of the willows,' Ohasu sang; and Oyuki joined in at, 'Wetting my sleeves and the hems of my skirts, wetting the path as I walk on my weeping way;' then Osome also came in as they sang, 'Sad spring rain in the lonely sadness of the willows,' their plaited voices rising, sweetly melancholy within the flickering pink lattice of falling cherry petals and ignored by the merchant poets who sprawled on the red felt mats and discussed forward contracts and funding strategies, sipping at their wine cups and helping themselves to fish salad, the sea bream being particularly tasty.

The sound of the bell fades, but the scent of blossoms continues: an evening.

OSOME WAS CARRIED OFF amidst great hilarity, the merchants promising to bedazzle her with night cherries illuminated by fires in iron baskets placed beneath the blossoming boughs. It was a famous spectacle, but Old

Master Bashō chose to stay behind at the picnic site with the two remaining peony girls.

Ohasu had been waiting for an opportunity to reminisce with her old teacher and perhaps discuss her recent efforts at *haikai* linked poetry. She had not brought copies with her – that would have been presumptuous – but she had memorised those she liked best and was prepared to recite them for him, should he ask her. She had also thought she might be invited to participate in the thirty-six stanza linked poem they were going to make, but that too hadn't happened.

The merchants had not lingered over the composition of their under-the-trees sequence. Profit came from steady accumulation, and they had added stanza after stanza with the casual ease of boys tossing pebbles into a cistern. Old Bashō had made suggestions for improvements occasionally, rewording awkward phrases and rejecting those for which no meaning could be found; but the finished poem had in the end suited the aesthetic requirements of the fee-payers, and the old poet sat alone and stared glumly out at the undulating river, the futility of his desire to convey the ineffable unnoticed by those who were satisfied at saying what was easily said.

The evening breeze had risen at sunset, and the surface of the red felt ground mat was littered with cherry petals. Drifts had collected in pink curds against the food containers and the trunk of their tree, and they continued to fall steadily so that by the following morning, the trees would be bare and the precious season over for another year.

The old poet's cup was empty so Ohasu came over and poured for him. She wondered if there wasn't something amiss in making an under-the-trees linked poem that flitted so lightly across the beauty of the nature of things.

Does it matter?

She had thought there would be more substance to it.

There was as much as they wanted.

But were you satisfied?

Old Bashō told her that his satisfaction was not the issue. He said he had been anticipating this moment of the year, determined to find the one perfect way of saying what he truly felt about it. But nothing had occurred to him. Every phrase he'd considered, every thought he'd had, had seemed to him like stealing garments from a dead man. His words were things remembered, phrases borrowed from what he'd read; and for that reason, anything he wrote would fail to describe what he had seen. Which meant he had not really seen it. So he wrote nothing. And felt like he never would again.

Ohasu sat frowning uncertainly. You don't mean that, she said.

You're telling me what I mean? The old poet dank then held out his wine cup to be refilled. If you love something within the language you use to describe it, then isn't what you love just the words?

But there's such a pleasure in fitting them together, creating new ways of expressing all the old –

I remember you. You think I don't?

Just that you hadn't said anything about the times that we –

Nothing to say. What? You want to talk about the past? Live it again?

No, Ohasu said, abashed.

You think I haven't felt what you feel? You think I don't remember what it's like?

Ohasu stared down at her hands and said nothing.

We can't be what we were, Bashō continued harshly. And what we are isn't worth having.

That's discouraging, Ohasu said.

Meant to be. And that was all he would say about the matter.

The merchants returned, Osome tripping along with them, her sash loose and the bodice of her gaudy robe flopping open; and the old poet left soon after receiving his fee.

Ohasu sat with the wine pourers; and when Oyuki began to play *Spring Banners*, she stood and began dancing as her friend stroked out the popular old ballad of longing and regret, mouthing the words of love betrayed as she swayed within the blowing swirls of falling cherry blossoms.

Ohasu danced for the day that was ending, for the tree being stripped and all the other trees along the riverbank also losing their blossoms. She danced for the urgency of the broad river flowing through the shogun's new city, and for the deepening blue of the evening sky and the darker green of the pines on the far shore. She danced for what she had lost and for what she would continue to lose, for what she had wished for and knew now would always be denied her. She danced for the husband she would not have, the children she would never bear, and for the comforting chatter of grandchildren in old age that would not be hers. And she danced for what she could have, the pleasure she found in the moment as it was. She felt the music in her hips and thighs, felt the dance pulling her earthwards, with the lightness of her hands opposing the weight of the music dragging her body downwards, death's promise being that even those who die alone have also once been alive.

Only briefly above the blossoming trees: tonight's moon.

Lightness

軽み

Old Master Bashō was dead, and there was no one to take his place. The gate to his cottage would be shut, the rain shutters attached, and *haikai* poets who had once sought his advice and approval would disperse like dry leaves blown in a gale. It was with this in mind that the senior Tokugawa retainer Sotobayama Ox-Blossom set off on a foot journey, intending to complete one final duty to the memory of his teacher. He did not wear robes of mourning, judging such displays presumptuous; but he did write the Old Master's death poem on his sedge-grass travel hat:

Ill while travelling, in my dreams still wandering over withered moors.

By late afternoon of the second day, he had reached the river-town which marked the outside boundary of the wide Musashi grasslands. The vermillion portal of the local *inari* shrine was guarded by a pair of stone fox statues wearing faded red votive bibs, and inside the sanctuary were mated pairs of miniature terracotta foxes arrayed on shelves, with shards of broken ones littering the floor tiles. A rattle-rope hung from the peak of the eaves. Ox-Blossom gave it a perfunctory shake to acknowledge the god's presence then returned to the shrine gardens. The stone purification trough was fed continuously by a bamboo trickle-pipe, and after rinsing his face and neck and forearms he settled on a bench and sat staring at the flat surface of water shimmering in the sunlight, overflow spilling out evenly on all sides of the rectangular trough and dribbling down the mossy flanks of stone.

On the day before his departure from Edo, a generous sum of cash money had been packed in a box and delivered to the proprietor of an assignations teahouse in the pleasure quarters. The Sotobayama-clan samurai who carried out this task had also been charged with conveying to the house-master what might happen should he behave in ways other than as was to be expected. The message was grasped. Ownership of her self was returned to the little peony girl who had been Ox-blossom's most recent friend.

The satisfaction of doing for another what she could not do for herself filled Ox-Blossom with tenderness and nostalgia and regret. They had parted badly. Poor little Okei had been left kneeling before him in the blue dawn, a gaudy robe draped over her naked shoulders as she told him she didn't know what she had done wrong. It had pained him at the time; and he had written in his prose journal about the emotions he felt, devising apt phrases and cunningly-wrought sentences. He liked what he made. He felt it displayed an appreciation of the poignancy of disappointment, as well as of the necessity to embrace the inevitability of the sadness of love lost, love betrayed, love undone by the dust of the world. All things considered, it was more than worth the suffering involved; and he tucked it away, pleased with himself.

The Sotobayama family were one of the most prominent in the Tokugawa bureaucracy although Ox-blossom's contribution was seldom praised. A dreamy man fond of poetry and old tales, he was slow to decide and even slower to act. His nickname had been attached to him in temple school because his ponderous way of copying out characters was said to be like that of a boy pressing words into sheets of drying mud. You're as slow as a plodding ox, one of his fellow pupils had hissed at him. Maybe so, the boy had replied. But on festival days, oxen are garlanded with the best blossoms.

Ox-blossoms! his fellow pupils had laughed; and the name had become so established that he accepted it as his poetry name too, finding a samurai's pride in the pose of self-effacement.

Ox-Blossom would have preferred to excuse himself from the task of editing the *haikai* group's final compendium. But others had already begun to define Old Master Bashō's way of linking in terms they could use to promote their own affairs. They wanted secret teachings, a catalogue of enigmas, a codification of arcane rules and requirements to which they could restrict access. Most would keep silent during the forty-nine days of deep mourning. But schismatics had already begun campaigning for a return to the 'profound-depth' style of linked poetry in repudiation of the 'lightness' of the Old Master's late manner, and only Ox-Blossom's prestige as a senior Tokugawa official could prevent them from taking over the valedictory publication entirely.

Once he had rested, Ox-Blossom continued out through the tenth-day market that was arranged along the banks of the river. Old Master Bashō had described this market in one of his last travel journals, and Ox-Blossom wished to see it through the eyes of his teacher. Yet as he watched itinerant pedlars pick through heaps of late-winter cabbages, checking for worm damage and leaf burn and the depredations of fungal rot – aware that their own customers would do the same – whatever lightness might be found in the scene was lost on him. No doubt an intensified under-standing was required, an appreciation of nuance that he seemed not to possess.

At the river ferry's quay Ox-Blossom paid his cop-per and joined the other passengers. A young wife with a pale complexion took the seat beside him. She was well-dressed for someone living in such a rural district; and she carried a pheasant cock in a woven bamboo basket-cage, the bird's long tail feathers protruding through a gap in the weave. The young wife told him her husband had snared the pheasant in the moorlands that morning. She was on her way to the retirement villa of a connoisseur who would pay five silver for the opportunity to paint a true image of it.

Is that so? A true image?

He is an artist who creates the exact likeness of what he sees placed before his eyes, and who condemns as frivolous the city painters in Edo or Miyako, with their phoenixes and dragons and Chinese *kirin*.

A painter of integrity, said Ox-Blossom.

Stew it with ginger and onions in a sweet-wine

broth, called the front oarsman from his perch at the fore transom; and the young wife smiled and glanced at Ox-Blossom in a way that reminded him of how whenever poor little Okei had become amused by something, she would check surreptitiously to see if his dignity would permit him to share it.

Being in a narrow boat on a swift river made the young wife anxious; and as they caught the current, she distracted herself by describing how she was obliged to manage two small children, a flock of ducks, an aged father-in-law who wandered in the lanes and became confused, and a husband who, although enterprising, had a fondness for squandering his time and money in the wine shops and brothels of the provincial castle town. The ducks, in particular, were a burden to her. There's no end to the ways they find to sicken and die, she said.

A difficulty indeed, said Ox-Blossom. He enjoyed seeing the new green of maples and liquidambars on the near shore sliding past, and the first traces of blooming cherries reminded him of the gaudy robes his little peony girl had worn, her nape exposed and the hem of her scarlet underskirt showing.

They will eat mouldy grain and collapse from bloating.

Is that so?

And rapeseed meal! How can they be so stupid as to eat something that poisons them?

A difficult question indeed…

His purchase of her contract had meant his little peony girl could now live anywhere, and he had won-

dered what Okei would do to support herself and instructed his house steward to keep track of her once she
left the pleasure quarters. He did not necessarily require further access himself – the acceptance of necessity being a point of pride with him – but he was curious about her fate.

I would imagine you have heard of the tail-bobbing
disease? said the young wife.

Tail bobbing?

Wheezing is another symptom.

I see, said Ox-Blossom thoughtfully.

Maggoty vent, too, although by then it's too late.

His little peony girl had told him once of her hope
to learn a useful skill. Her father had been a scribe in
service to the Tokugawa family, and Okei was an excel-
lent calligrapher although she had no interest in linked
poetry. He had enjoyed the way her little pink tongue
protruded between her lips as she concentrated on
writing out lines of text, and he wondered if some use
for her writing abilities might not be found.

And castor beans! Do not say a word to me about
castor beans!

No. But he had to say something. You raise them for
their eggs then?

Eggs and feathers for now. Then later duck meat.
The wife's small face shone serenely, all fear of the
swollen river current forgotten. I will get a good price
in the city.

You will take them there yourself?

I will. For my husband would not make it past the
first wine shop.

A difficult situation.

Difficult, yes. But she would be the one in the city visiting the new dry goods emporiums with cash money to spend while her husband remained behind in the village, with one snivelling child tied on his back and the other stumbling along whining for his suck dummy. An obi in the new, extra-wide style will be my first purchase, and perhaps even a gaudy robe like the kind they wear in the pleasure quarters.

I see.

And tortoiseshell hair ornaments, mottled yellow and brown. I know exactly the ones I want.

Indeed. And he too knew them, decorations like those his little peony girl had shown him shyly; and it occurred to Ox-Blossom that this too was a kind of lightness, these ordinary correspondences, things as they were without embellishment.

Ox-Blossom had always assumed that he under-stood Old Master Bashō's way of linking in his late manner because his descriptions of it were so simple. In fact, all he'd done was understand the words he had used. But now as he was able at last to recall with tran-quility his days and nights of doubt and desire in the pleasure quarters, he detected within his reconfigura-tion of what had been endured an abrupt easing of the pain of separation, like the moment when after a pro-tracted struggle, the curved worm is at last extracted from the tight spiral of the winkle shell.

And clogs with scarlet toe cords! Can you imagine?

He could; and after wishing the young wife a safe journey, he set off on the road to the remote mountain villa where the final edit of the Bashō Group Compendium would be made, hiking up through the moist heat of early spring until he reached a roadside rest shelter. He drank from his water gourd then held it cradled in his palms, the damp surface slick as catfish skin. The idea of the sadness of lost love was in many ways more satisfying than the peony girl herself had been. He drank again then got out his writing kit and sketched a prose heading:

The true image of things: a bird in a cage and a skiff on a river. What else is there but this? Unsure of my feelings, and unable to seek the advice of my little friend left behind in Edo, I devised this poor offering for her.

Then he dashed off a quick *hokku* opening-stanza, the words dropping down each out of the one before in a single, sinuous line of black ink:

Clogs with scarlet toe cords left under a cherry tree; spring arrives in the barrier mountains.

THE CLOUD TERRACE PAVILION was a medieval villa perched high on the southernmost peaks of the mountains that formed the central spine of the main island of the archipelago. It had been constructed by a family whose descendants chose the wrong side during the civil war, resulting in the slaughter of their persons and the forfeiture of their estates. In the decades that followed the establishment of the Tokugawa Great Peace, the Cloud Terrace had become a favourite venue for connoisseurs in search of the subtleties of the pleasures of the past. The main structure was a large, open-sided pavilion with a massive roof of slate-grey tiles. An external porch thrust out over the void was supported by a trestlework of pillars, each pier of which was fashioned from a whole cedar tree. Attendant buildings and cottages were dispersed among the surrounding groves and crags. Covered walkways connected the complex together so that upright granite scarps and dramatically twisted pines formed part of the architecture.

Aesthetes were drawn to the Cloud Terrace by its simulation of a way of life that had long since ended, and the villa's Tokugawa masters – susceptible themselves to the lure of nostalgia and the seductions of self-indulgence – ensured that no hint of modernity obtruded in any obvious way. The cushions, screen paintings, tray tables and crockery were recent masterworks modelled on cherished originals; and the robes issued to guests were self-consciously archaic although newly made from fine silks and satins, authenticity of effect being more important to the Tokugawa than actual authenticity.

Ox-Blossom was met by his fellow editors in the main assembly hall. You have been here for a few days then?

We have indeed. Some arrived yesterday, others the day before. You are our only laggard.

The pleasure providers selected for the occasion of the final edit complemented the furnishings by radiating an aura of sweet wistfulness. Their hair was styled in an antique manner and their eyebrows plucked out to create the broad smooth forehead of the classic Heian beauty. They were costumed in seven layers of silk

robes, the combinations of colours where they over-
lapped at the sleeves and bodice openings meant to ex-
emplify the elegance of that earlier age; and they hid
themselves simpering behind robe-draped screens and
veiled their faces when on outings amidst the cliffs and
grottoes or even when transiting between buildings,
their timidity considered charmingly erotic although
this semblance of reluctance was set aside during the
long and liquid banquets that filled the afternoons and
evenings at the terrace – the managing of modesty-veils
during such celebrations judged an intolerable nuisance
– and abandoned wholly during night frolics in the
outdoor thermal baths, when the illusion of the disin-
clination felt by refined ladies to exposed themselves to
the gaze of the world dissolved in the rustic ambience
of sulphurous fumes and hot water.

Stacked against the inside wall of the main pavilion
building were panniers filled with hand scrolls, printed
books, bound manuscripts, and bundle upon bundle of
loose sheaves of poems tied together with silk cords. A
few of the panniers had been opened already and their
contents arranged in piles of association although this
seemed premature since criteria of assessment had not
yet been determined. Ox-Blossom was prepared to defend 'lightness' as an ideal, and he knew that others
would support him; but the cabal of poets who wished
to return to the 'profound-depth' style of linked poetry
would make demands requiring compromise and even,
Ox-blossom knew, the occasional capitulation.

The first day was spent sorting the vast array of ma-
terials. The editors spread themselves around the large

pavilion, some choosing the outer edge with its views of the misty spring sky and distant mountains, others preferring the inner ambience of gardens and grottoes. Senior Editor Ox-Blossom occupied the central position in front of the *tokonoma* alcove. A *haiga* painting by their teacher hung there, depicting a brush-wood gate with a plantain growing beside it. Before it stood an upright Korean vase containing a single spray of mountain cherry blossoms. The pleasure providers served as messengers, carrying scrolls and manuscripts between editors and scribes, their mounds of silk robes rustling as they moved about the large open-air pavilion, conveying questions and comments and, upon occasion, clever witticisms which they pretended not to understand and often didn't.

In the middle of the room three piles were established: one for poems and linking stanzas that had been accepted, one for the obvious rejects, and one for those still undecided, with a rationale for each decision entered into a log which could be reviewed should disputes arise later.

By the end of the afternoon, the sorting process had been completed. The undecided pile was larger than the senior editor would have preferred, but he had won debates he'd anticipated losing and retained submissions he'd thought doomed. Disputatious camps had formed within the 'return to profundity' clique; small differences had become magnified; egos had swollen; and certain attributes of the profound manner of *haikai* linked poetry had so risen in importance in the minds of its defenders that the acrimony which billowed up around the appropriateness of including the image of a pine tree in a vision of autumn hills trembling with coloured leaves seethed violently, grew in intensity, and almost destroyed the work that had gone before as one group of disgruntled conservatives threatened to renounce all further co-operation and return immediately to Edo if such grotesque aesthetic deformities weren't repudiated. A compromise was reached finally, and an otherwise inoffensive poem about weepy lovers watching the wake of a boat disappear into swirling mist was sacrificed in a gesture of amelioration.

The day's work done, some of the poet-editors hiked up to a small viewing platform perched higher in the mountains while others strolled down to the thermal baths, where a few of the bolder pleasure providers were known to be awaiting them, naked as peeled willow wands in the soft spring air. Only the senior editor remained on the terrace, assisted by a scribe and the youngest and least experienced of the pleasure providers, a weedy little creature whose nose was pink with inflammation.

Ox-Blossom was near the end of his review of the submissions still in dispute when he came to a single hand scroll containing a series of linked poems that he had composed one afternoon while visiting his lost peony girl. He scanned through the sequence until he found one that Okei had liked and recited it to the girl kneeling forlornly in the corner.

She said she thought it was nice.

And this? He read another of Okei's favourites.

It's nice too, replied the young pleasure provider, twin pearls of mucus expanding and contracting on the bottom rims of her nostrils as she sniffled in quick little snorts.

Ox-Blossom wondered if those stanzas didn't characterise his teacher's late manner better than his more sophisticated efforts did. He held the scroll for a moment longer then placed it on the alcove shelf behind him rather than consigning it to one of the piles in the middle of the room.

The evening banquet began with rare delicacies, and it rumbled forward in a spirit of fellowship. Wine flowed and agreements were reached, ruffled feathers smoothed, slights forgotten. The night wore on to its conclusion with some matters left unresolved, however. Was, or was not, low diction to be condemned? All recognised the factuality of a nightingale shitting on rice cakes on a veranda, but was that in itself sufficient? The celebrants pondered the imponderable, held their wine cups up to be refilled, and eventually tottered off to the various cottages and pavilions they had been assigned, some accompanied by pleasure providers and some not.

Ox-Blossom ordered paper lanterns placed along the path leading out to one of the more secluded thermal pools. Pale wisps of steam rose from the dark surface of the sulphurous water and dissolved into the inky blackness of the night's sky. He hung his clothing on the stubs of branches on a nearby pine which had been trimmed for that purpose then used the old-fashioned dipping gourd to rinse himself and warm his skin before settling into the murky pool, clutching himself against the heat of the water. The spring night was clear and bright with stars, and the uncertain young pleasure provider stood hovering obediently in the glow of the nearest paper lantern. She said everybody else was tucked in their quilts. She said she didn't know what she was supposed to do. She said she was called the Princess of the Chamber of the Fragrance of Lilies although that wasn't her real name; and she struggled with the multiple layers of her unfamiliar costume and the various sashes and ties that held it all together, searching out a separate branch stub for each garment so that the edge of the thermal pool took on an exotic ambience, with the silk robes and underskirts and dangling sashes forming a polychrome backdrop to the austere simplicity of the mountain grotto.

The girl squatted at the edge of the pool. Judging it presumptive to touch a gourd dipper that had been used by the senior editor, she rinsed herself by splashing up palmfuls of water in a foolish and ineffective manner. She was a scrawny little thing, with a concave chest and nipples still those of a child, the patch of shame hair at her little jade gate hardly more than a tuft of black floss. She crept forward then sank into the hot water, emitting strangled little gasps of dismay at the shock of the heat of it, two lines of snot depending suddenly from her nostrils.

Ox-Blossom returned his attention to the silver river of stars flowing above them, the beauty of the milky flooding of it across the unimaginable depths of the spring night sky.

It's lovely up here in the mountains, he said, and the

fragrant princess responded with a constricted squeak of assent.

Had she been here before?

She had not.

Probably you are unfamiliar with such gatherings.

She was unfamiliar with all things.

So a new experience for you, Ox-Blossom said in an avuncular manner; and when they retired to his personal chambers and the quilts spread there for them, he gave her instructions and gently corrected infelicities; then once one thing had led successfully to another, he asked if she couldn't stop snuffling at least long enough for him to fall asleep.

THE BATTLES THAT OX-BLOSSOM had anticipated were joined throughout the day of the final cull; he won some, he lost some, and some were left unresolved. With the content of the compendium largely determined, they could begin arranging the poems into sequences, a task that would take several more days, with the undecided submissions used to fill gaps.

In a moment of hubris, Ox-Blossom told the fragrant princess that when he returned to Edo, she would come with him, attached to his entourage, and a place would be found for her at the Sotobayama Family Compound, with appropriate duties and an older member of the household staff to look after her.

The banquet that second night was as sumptuous as had been the one the night before; and the good humour shared among the editors was sincere, for the conservatives had found in Ox-Blossom a tractable Tokugawa bureaucrat who would yield when pressed while Ox-Blossom himself felt that he had preserved enough of the poems in their Old Master's late manner to satisfy the requirements of his obligation. Celebratory wine cups were exchanged again and again, with the pleasures providers scrambling to fill and refill them; and there was a point late in the evening when Ox-Blossom suddenly grasped the truth of the manner of lightness. He sent for an inkstone and brush, and he retrieved the scroll of poems he had made with the peony girl and added a concluding stanza at the bottom:

A spring night and no one shares the sadness of what's been lost: silk robes draped forlornly on a pine tree.

That was it. The simple clarity of an honest emotion. And he smiled to think that if he hadn't lost his little peony girl, then such an understanding might never have occurred to him.

The fragrant princess gazed at her new benefactor from her place in the corner. Her coif was enhanced with a few additional silver baubles although her runny nose seemed unimproved, and Ox-blossom wondered for a moment if he hadn't been a bit precipitous in taking her into his service although of course corrections would always be an option.

Abnegation

克 己 心

The rogue samurai Hasegawa Torakage was still searching for the path he wanted when he chanced upon a collapsed gate lying in the weeds like some kind of primitive winnowing device discarded in a repudiation of husbandry. He pushed up through a forest of giant bamboo that was as thick as a man's leg, and came to a one-room shanty, the roof so burdened with moss and summer ferns and cloud-ears that its original shape could no longer be determined.

Mugen the Recluse sat half-naked on the veranda, a scrawny and filthy apparition, his tattered black monk's robe pushed down into a bundle wrapped around his waist. He slapped a mosquito then wiped the blood smear off his arm. Another new Buddha. He wiped his palm on the wad of his robe.

The walls of the Unreal Hermitage were plastered in places with mud patches crudely sheathed with strips of split bamboo. Neat pyramids of clay pellets lay beneath some of these renovations, as if in demonstration of the better order that could be achieved by insects gifted with enterprise and enthusiasm.

Hasegawa lifted his main sword from his obi sash

and leaned it against the side of the hermitage. You're hard to find, he said.

We all are.

They watched as the day seeped down out of the sky, and the last of the end-of-summer fireflies began wandering through the weeds of the derelict garden as tiny, tentative lamps that flared and faded then flared again.

'In the morning, damp rises up through holes in the floor,' Hasegawa recited; 'and in the evening, drizzle leaks down through gaps in the roof.'

Mugen snorted derisively. Just the kind of thing that impresses these ignorant old mountain monks.

Hasegawa smiled at him. Probably I should give it up.

Probably you'd be better off without it.

Probably I would be.

The evening's darkness settled more deeply around them. If I had any rice wine, I'd ask if you wanted some, said the recluse. And if you asked if I wanted some, I'd ask if you had any. But it wouldn't get us any closer to drinking.

No. Hasegawa watched the fireflies still bobbing in the garden, weaving their patterns of meaningless meanings, the designs they carved beyond any possibility of improvement. What I have is what I was born with. A cutter's expectations. The requirements of candour. Swords given to me by my father. His swords when he died. Swords taken off other dead men and –

Fierce poetry! Mugen cackled, and he seized both earlobes like a man with burnt fingers then began rocking from side to side, a holy-mad Daruma roller frowning at the comedy of the sham of the display. But so then tell me, O honoured killer, where's the wine after you drink it?

An owl flapped out across the open space at the far side of the abandoned garden, a shifting portion of that night's shadows differing only in intensity from the other shadows surrounding it, and the recluse released his earlobes as if in response to a reprimand.

Hasegawa waited until he was looking at him again then said, Where's the 'you' after the drinking?

Too easy! cried the recluse. I can see why you're still mystified. He scratched himself then grimaced like a wildwood bogey. Can you?

I guess not. Hasegawa returned his attention to the darkening bamboo forest. My life would be lonely if it weren't for the solitude?

Those are just words.

I know it. But where are your words without you saying them?

You read that somewhere. You have a bookish stink on you.

Hasegawa smiled. It's where I get most things I trust.

Off dead men.

Men of the past. Yes.

Nothing but mumbling! Mugen glared at the rogue samurai. You can't see how it is with the world of words? All tangled and strangled and knotted and bound? I'd rather be a shit-scraper hanging on a peg in a public latrine.

I guess that's true enough, said Hasegawa mildly, what you said, I mean. He grinned at him. The clever way you expressed it.

Still too easy, the recluse said although he sounded less sure of it. Words wobble. Fall over. Lie there looking up at you. He scratched at a mosquito bite on his arm, making it bleed, touched his tongue to the blood. Non-words do too, he said then shouted: You piss it out!

Hasegawa smiled. I used to want things. Then I thought I didn't. Now I don't know. He told the recluse how he had been wandering for over a hundred days, following along the lower slopes of the barrier mountains and seeking rigours for the body as mechanisms for measuring the resilience of the soul. Grass pillows and sky quilts. People said bears still live up there in the back country but I never saw one. Nor had he met any person who'd encountered such a beast. I went all the way around to the Western Coast Road, walking through the heat of the day and bivouacking wherever evening stopped me. Some nights I sang to the moon. Some I yelled curses at it. Finally got to a place where I could smell the sea and turned around and came back the way I'd gone. One direction as good as any other. So then I thought that if I –

Bear shit?

Bear shit?

See any?

He hadn't.

Know it if he saw it?

No. Probably not.

The recluse nodded to himself and plucked at the unravelling hem of his black robe. Where I learned to sit was at the Great Virtue Monastery in Miyako. Big old buildings full of shave-pates all pushing as hard as they can. Backs straight. Feet tucked in. Faces so still and solemn it would make a cat laugh just to look at us. Nobody could match me there.

I don't doubt it.

Ask about me. They'll tell you. Here's an iron-ass bonze who *will not move*!

They remained silent for a long moment, the myriad world outside lowering itself into a darkness that became one with the darkened interior of the ramshackle hermitage.

I thought I'd write about things as I saw them, said Hasegawa. Mountains and rivers, birds and flowers. But all I saw was what they meant. Not what they are.

More greed.

I guess that's so. Hasegawa pulled up his water gourd by its cord and took a drink. There were certain ways of behaving that samurai always accepted. But now that's no longer needed. The shogunate's a bureaucracy. They worry about what they look like, where they sit. Men who used to trust their blades now make entries in account books and are judged by the quality of their calligraphy.

Gone! Gone! The old happy days of slaughter!

Hasegawa laughed. He said he'd been raised to accept the inevitability of the fact of convergence. But then he too had picked up a writing brush and begun jotting down things in journals. He too went back over what he'd done and tried to devise ways of making it better. Carve a Buddha statue out of rotten wood. It's still a Buddha statue. But it's also still rotten.

All right. Mugen gazed around then said, You go knock on the gate of the Great Virtue just north-west of Old Miyako. They'll tell you about a wonder-bonze whose Zen roared like a blazing fire. He scratched violently in his armpit then examined what he had rooted out. Of course back then you'd also find this old fraud climbing over the monastery walls at night. Talk about greed!

You being him.

Me being stupid.

All right.

The topic being greed.

Hasegawa smiled. Meaning mine?

Meaning yours.

All right. He nodded at it. I still try to make things out of words, but they never seem true. So I try the words different ways. If I can't fix it, I throw it away. But I can't throw away what it should have been. So I keep that.

Try spitting straight up. Maybe you'll learn something.

All right. Hasegawa watched the drifting lamps of fireflies, the way they transformed the grasses and bushes of the overgrown garden into webs of transience, each tiny light disappearing then reappearing a certain distance from where it had extinguished itself. No walls for the ego's self to climb out here, he said.

Ask about the marvellous bonze they lost. They'll

tell you he could sit zazen all day and drink rice wine all night. Local whores called for him by name. You can still hear faint echoes of them shouting for joy: Hey, good girls! Come upstairs! Crazy old Mugen's riding his little pink pony tonight!

So your pride's still with you?

You can't keep what you write if you don't like the *words*?

Hasegawa thought about it then said, You can describe the world as being simpler than it is, and a reader will take comfort in your easy answers. Good is rewarded, evil punished, and lost children are restored to their mothers. Or you can declare how it's impossible to say anything really true about the world, and your reader will think you're a profound fellow with deep thoughts. Or you can say no. Here it is. This is it. And press at what you find and press and press at it until you push through to the original beauty of things, and those readers who persevere will follow you into the mysterious depths of the true essence of being.

Well! The recluse bonze leaned to the side, lifted one scrawny buttock, and released a long slow sonorous fart of remarkable resonance and duration.

Hasegawa laughed. I guess you don't agree. He stroked the weather-worn boards of the veranda, scraping together seeds that had blown up there, feeling a pile take shape under his fingertips. I showed some of what I'd written to Old Master Bashō. He made a few corrections, said he thought it wasn't entirely hopeless.

All right. So then that's what you have. Red marks on sheets black with ink.

Hasegawa squared-up his seed pile then started another.

So here's mine. One hot summer day some good few years ago, the much admired Zen-hammer Mugen left the Old Imperial City of Miyako. Birds wept to see him go, and the eyes of fish were filled with tears. A golden nimbus shone around the noble bonze as he hiked without wavering into the forest, left foot right foot, left foot right foot, straight as a shot arrow. Went right on through blocking bushes and tangling vines, streams and rocks and trees no obstacle. Where he had been became where he wasn't. Finally he reached here. A nameless place without people.

Hasegawa nodded but said nothing.

But you probably want to know why he never went back to the Great Virtue. He might tell you he got tired of city dust, but that's not true. He liked the dust, liked to stir it, stick his man-stick in. And you might think they wouldn't have him with all his hopping fleas and crawling lice. But that's not it either. They wanted him back for his big loud Zen. So finally a delegation of delegates came out full of words, but the wonder-bonze wouldn't listen. They left some things in the garden. Robes and sandals and books and begging bowls and cooking pots and knives and ladles and sieves. Once autumn passes and the weeds die back, you'll see bits of it sticking up.

I don't understand.

It's a story.

A story.

And yours is too.

The moon rose out of the blackness behind them, silvering the tops of the giant bamboo so that they glittered like the surface of the sea as seen from below. Hasegawa said, So then I guess you don't think you're free from the chain of unavoidable consequences...

The recluse bonze scratched himself. You don't listen very well, do you.

No. I guess not.

Tree frogs had begun proposing an agenda for that night, the single voice starting it soon joined by others, braiding in various opinions and refinements until the possibilities that had accumulated formed a tapestry so rich in its implications that a moment's silence was required for the song-weavers to ponder the marvel of their design.

Women and words and reputations, said the recluse. Can I learn not to want the encumbrances of this world? I can learn it!

But it's harder not to want the not-wanting, Hasegawa said, his face again turned towards the bobbing lamps of fireflies, their numbers beginning to decline as their brief evening ended. Walking. Remembering. Writing. Walking...

And you think that's good enough?

Hasegawa sat on the edge of the veranda, the moon's radiance leaking down into the darkening ligature of the bamboo forest, filling the weedy garden, silvering the blank mountains beyond, all the world everywhere holding itself much the way fingers might be cupped on the hands of someone cradling new-born kittens. I guess even a needle-thief can dream of spears.

MUGEN'S METHOD WAS A SERIES of abrupt adjustments, with each choice yielding the easier route. They pushed up through the giant bamboo then began climbing into the cedar forest on the higher slopes. At about the hour of the horse, they reached an island of exposed granite. They drank from their water gourds then lay on their backs on the sun-flooded rock and watched a hawk tilting directly above them, gripping the air with an easy grace.

The recluse bonze sat up and unstopped his water gourd again. You ever hear the story about how old Nansen taught the truth of the dharma?

No.

Well, then. This old-time abbot Nansen, he –

No.

No?

No.

He looked at him. You decided you don't like stories?

Hasegawa said there were times when a person didn't want to hear explanations, teachings, anecdotes, and that for him this was one of those times, or was about to become so.

Seems to me one time is the same as any other, said the recluse, and he drank then tapped the gourd stopper back in place.

They continued hiking uphill through the middle part of the day then came to an elongated alpine dell filled with jade-green mountain ferns and ending against an abrupt backdrop of limestone cliffs. Mugen waded in then flopped over backwards, rolling in the ferns with his elbows flapping, carving a space for himself like some kind of mud-monkey flushed up into the open air. At the other end, he said. You go all the way back. Mugen's eyes were closed and he breathed in deeply, filling himself with the scent and sensation of the crushed ferns. See that jumble of rocks? There's a path there.

The sheer upright expanse of gray limestone was fractured into irregular pinnacles and palisades. Seepage darkened the surface of the stone, and at the base lay a tumble of mossy boulders that had once been part of the cliff face. Hasegawa climbed up to the entrance of the limestone grotto. Hewn blocks of cliff-rock formed the front walls and entryway portal, the surfaces smoothed from centuries of wind and rain, as if the upright pilaster-supports and the massive horizontal stone forming the lintel were being reabsorbed into the mountain itself.

The floor of the cavern was slippery and slanted downward. He moved to the side wall and felt his way along the wet stone surface as his eyes adjusted to the gloom. The air was damp and cool and smelled of dust and decay. He went deeper then left the side wall and crept forward, peering into the blackness. A broad shelf ran along the back wall of the grotto, carved directly out of the flanks of the mountain and serving as a crude altar. No candlesticks or incense burners were to be found there, no stacked sutras or bowls of crystal fruit or vases of porcelain lotus blossoms. Only the array of seated images showed that this was a place meant for worship. Hasegawa went from one to the next. Gaunt human figures spaced apart on the shelf sat rigidly up-right and frozen in full lotus position, implacable in their insistence and awful to behold. Some would have been there for hundreds of years, others were more recent. But each of the Followers of the Way of Perfected Abnegation had achieved a state of unwavering self-mortification that transcended the stench of the flesh of the world, their faces dried to skin-covered skulls, their leathery bellies sunken to hollows beneath out-bowed rib cages, their dry arms and legs little more than sinewy sticks so that every bone and ligature seemed bound within the preservative of death's own sheathing.

Hasegawa studied the face of the avatar located at the deepest end of the shelf, trying to detect some glimmer of meaning in the two blind patches of dried shadow that obscured what had once been eyes, the nose crumpled like a withered walnut, the pale wedges of a few remaining teeth. He held up a down feather, moving it closer and closer to the grimacing lips until he could confirm a slight fibrillation.

Hasegawa placed one hand on the knee of the desiccated creature and held it there, asking nothing and giving nothing and only confirming what he had always known. Then he turned away and went back out to the light of the high autumn sky framed by the trees of the forest, and the recluse bonze still wallowing in his nest of crushed ferns.

He sat down beside him.

The recluse waited long enough to be sure his silence was intentional then said, Maybe you didn't look hard enough.

They hiked back downhill, not mentioning the grotto of the perfected mountain ascetics nor discussing any other such topics until they were seated on the ramshackle veranda of the Unreal Hermitage, once again watching the gathering dusk as it began seeping into the bamboo grove.

Probably you could say, why should I search for what I haven't lost? And then I would say, how can you know whether you've lost it if you don't know what it is?

Hasegawa said nothing then he said, It seems wrong.

So maybe you were just *curious*? Is that the way it is with you? Wondering what it's *like*?

Hasegawa studied the bright surfaces of the bamboo trunks still holding the last gleam of twilight within the darkness, unsure what to propose and unhappy with what occurred to him.

You taper off, the recluse said. Rice gruel and pickles. Then just tree ears and fern shoots. Nuts and berries and certain mountain plants. For years and years. Then no plants, then no berries. As you get closer, you shift to certain barks. The tannin helps preserve the skin. Then just pine needles. Then just the tips of pine needles. Then just the points of the tips. Then just the prick of them.

All right.

Then just the memory of it. The recluse slapped at his bare shoulder then smeared the blood spot off his palm. Another Buddha. Born of my hand. He smirked like an offer-maker burdened by an obtuse audience then said, I guess just because it doesn't mean much, which side of the line you're on. Other than that there's a line.

That sounds like something made out of words, Hasegawa said. But he wasn't satisfied with it and didn't know why.

'Rats occupy the four corners,' Mugen intoned. 'A wasp nest hangs under the roof beam. And spiders and beetles and centipedes circulate throughout the room, and do whatever they desire...'

Hasegawa nodded, recognising the quote. So then you too try?

I try not to try.

Just point at it?

Finding the traces before seeing the ox.

It's still the same. Anecdotes. Stories. Lessons. Everything's made out of words. Hasegawa said nothing for a moment then said, I guess what I don't understand is why I don't feel any better about knowing that.

Maybe because you don't know it yet.

Maybe not.

Whatever they are, and whatever you think about them and their yearning for perfection, what *they* did is not made out of words!

No. I know that. He sat gazing into the autumn twilight. But it's also just becoming dead as slowly as possible. Like trying to watch it happen. A kind of greed.

Mugen scowled then grinned and shook himself like a water-spaniel back on dry land. So then what in your honour's opinion did you encounter in there?

Dead men dying in a hole, Hasegawa said harshly. With no *reason* for it.

The recluse laughed. And so we confirm once again that your samurai values still hold you.

I've cut men and I'm sorry about it. But there are also some I'm not sorry about. And I don't know what else to say.

I guess that's all right then.

But it was mockery and Hasegawa thought he deserved it. No, he said. It isn't.

The recluse observed him. You ever tell the truth?

Hasegawa looked back at him blankly.

I mean, to yourself?

I knew what you meant, Hasegawa said.

So then what will you say to the man who kills you?

You mean if I'm not him?

All right.

Hasegawa returned his attention to the settling night, the beauty of the way shadows flowed out from dark pockets into lighter planes. I don't know, he said. I don't see how that's the kind of thing you can know.

But you'd kill another man. If there was a reason for it.

I guess I would.

They sat together silently for a long moment, then the recluse said, I didn't try to teach you anything. What he had offered was to point out something that the rogue samurai might learn on his own. But you didn't see it, Mugen said. And the following morning, bright and early, he guided him down through the bamboo forest to a path that led around the edge of a swampy meadow and would join up with the main road. Morning sunlight bathed the reeds and water grasses growing there, and small white butterflies filled the air, fluttering around each other like bits of torn paper dancing. Hasegawa continued alone out into the open wash of autumn sunlight, his feet sinking into the swampy earth, releasing the fragrance of it. He stopped then came back. I guess you forgot to give me your lesson. Probably the fault is mine.

Probably.

So?

So anyway, a long time ago, there was this old abbot in China named Nansen and he knew a lot. Could answer your question before you even asked it. Had a stick to hit you with when the lesson required direct intervention. So anyway, one day one of his lip-flapping monks got a little too close and the stick-whack dropped him to his knees. If there's a dharma truth no one has professed yet? old Nansen shouted out. Isn't that what you're wondering? Well, yes, there is one! The lip flapper rubbed his sore head and said nothing. Old Nansen told him he wanted to know about it. The lip flapper moved back to where it was safer then admitted that he did. And old Nansen spoke up with a voice that shook like thunder and said, This is not the mind. This is not the Buddha nature. This is not a distinction between being and non-being.

Mugen's mouth gaped open and he leaned forward, staring intently into the face of the rogue samurai. Don't you want to know what the 'this' is?

You forget to bring your stick?

I need one I'll borrow yours.

Nor is that any answer either.

Nor would there ever be one.

Hasegawa smiled. He gazed around at the swampy moorland, the unfolding scent of living mud heating under the morning sun. Nevertheless, it's our nature to wish to praise it, he said, the world as it is. And he told him he acknowledged the truths of the transmitted doctrines and revered them. He said he knew he was at fault and would continue to be so; and Mugen watched him depart then turned away himself and scampered back into the bamboo forest, an absurd and filthy apparition slapping at the upright trunks of giant bamboo for the joy of the sound that made and the feel of the hollow smack against his palm.

A Gap on the Wall
壁 の 間

A signboard posted at the entry plaza listed the rules for using the Great Bridge. Fires were strictly forbidden. No vending was allowed up there, no begging or carnal solicitation. It was not permitted to throw anything off the bridge. Shitting on it was a punishable offence, and care should be used when pissing over the side on windy days. Bullocks were denied access but horses were allowed. Removing planks or railings or any portion of the bridge or its fittings or fixtures was a crime, as was building any structure on it or under it. Ohasu found all these requirements sensible.

But I wish you were going with me...

I wish I was too, Oyuki had said.

The incline was steep where the bridge connected to the embankment. Loaded carts on the downward slopes were hard to restrain, and carters yelled at careless persons who seemed about to wander into their path. Ohasu was determined not to make any foolish blunders that would betray her as a novice bridge-crosser. When you're out alone in the world you need to behave like you belong where you are, Oyuki had advised her. Even if you're lost.

Ohasu's possessions were packed in a large carry-sack tied onto her back like a pedlar, and she wore rice-straw sandals as the best choice for the walking road and a broad cypress-bark rain hat with a wayfarer's incantation written on it by a previous owner. Her robe was mouse grey with a grey under-pattern of elongated lozenges, and her obi sash was equally modest; but her only underskirts were the bright scarlet silk garments worn in the pleasure quarters so she took care when stepping over obstacles not to display too much. People watch you and you may not be aware of what they're really thinking.

A cart piled high with bales of rice came rumbling and roaring down off the bridge with a sound like thunder. The back men strained to slow it with drag-ropes, and the front men were leaning against the weight of it, their eyes wide and their heels bleeding.

They always do that like that, said a man with a load of dried squid on a carry-pole; although whether he meant it as praise or condemnation was unclear to Ohasu.

The Lesser Tada had asked if she wanted to burn her contract herself. In addition to the purchase of her person, a certain amount of cash money had also been bequeathed to her; and the assignations-teahouse owner counted it out slowly, building up piles of coins in groups of tens, as if hoping that she might offer to return some of it to him in a gesture of forgiveness. You keep every copper for yourself, Oyuki had advised her, and she did.

Once she reached mid-span, Ohasu tucked in close against the bridge rail for the view of the river far below. Seagulls slid above the undulating surface of the water and occasionally passed under the bridge itself. It had never occurred to her that flying birds could be seen from above. What a wonder and a marvel, and as she leaned out over the bridge railing giddy with the novelty of height, a coastal lighter emerged from directly beneath her, its mast weirdly foreshortened and oscillating widely, the sailors reduced to the tops of their heads.

Ohasu would have liked to write something memorializing her awe at what she was seeing; but she hurried on her way, unwilling to put at risk the successful completion of her first bridge crossing.

Before she left Edo, Ohasu had visited the mansion of her deceased benefactor and asked to see the old man's beloved iris beds. All had been dug up and discarded, the mansion's new owners having other plans for the gardens. As she walked back from the front gate, Ohasu had come upon a mound of withered iris plants abandoned in a waste ground and sorted through the rhizomes, selecting those she judged most viable. What you have is what you do in this world, Oyuki had said to her, and not what is done to you.

But, still, she wished she could have thanked him.

But perhaps she had. Probably he had understood her true feelings.

Houses and shops and storehouses had been established on the far shore of the river, clustered around a memorial temple erected to soothe the souls of those who perished in urban fires. A woman travelling alone couldn't be admitted, but a novice monk followed

Ohasu outside then led her around to an annex shed where extra winter quilts were stored. If it wasn't allowed it also wasn't forbidden. He lit a paper lantern for her and placed it inside the doorway. There was a cistern in the garden at the back, suitable for bathing.

Ohasu thanked him for his kindness.

The novice returned after the evening bell. He had brought a bowl of rice gruel with strips of fried tofu and a little dish of yellow pickles and a pot of tea. He carried the tray awkwardly and didn't seem to know where to put it so she showed him. He said he would not be able to sit with her for fear of distracting himself, and she praised his determination and thanked him again for his generosity.

The novice stood in the doorway, his hands fumbling together like squid mating. She hadn't bathed yet.

Ohasu lifted the lid off the bowl of rice gruel. No.

Just that it's safe enough back there is all. The water in the cistern is clean. And he would make certain no one tried to watch her.

She held the lid then placed it neatly beside the bowl. You're very kind.

But I can't sit with you. Not because I'm so weak. But she was obviously an innocent young girl who would be susceptible to temptation.

You're very kind to think of me, said Ohasu.

The ways of men in this world are various.

Indeed they are. But he himself was proof that desire could be resisted.

The novice nodded in vague agreement with this; and he returned again at the hour of the boar, wishing to convince Ohasu that she was in no peril there and to encourage her to make use of the restorative properties of the cistern, describing again the route one followed, the ease of lighting the path with a hand lantern, and the efficiency of positioning that lantern near the water source by perhaps hanging it from the limb of a tree where one's clothing also could be hung. She thanked him again. But her long day's walk had left her too tired to bathe.

I see. He watched her. No doubt your legs are not strong yet.

No doubt that is the case.

And your body is also of a small size.

Yes. Ohasu regarded him, waiting.

Your hips are narrow as a boy's. And your thighs seem quite slender...

Ohasu awoke with the pre-dawn bell and departed, dropping a few coppers in the offertory box. By the time the rising sun had cleared the rim of the eastern hills, she was in farmland. A low white mist still clung to the fields, and the dewy roadside grass wetted her hems. I'm going home, Ohasu told everyone she met. To see my mother.

Her road lead through rice fields being drained in preparation for harvest, the dark yellow rice heads bowed over by their own weight; and she paused at the sight of two red dragonflies attached to the tops of reeds growing in a water channel, one higher than the other, the redness of them intense against the bright hard blue of the autumn sky. She followed the water channel back to where it fed down from a hillside stream and planted one of her irises there. She had thought she might say a prayer to aid the transmigration of her patron's soul, but the planting itself seemed enough. Later that morning she found another good spot for her rhizomes near a woman who was squatting at the edge of a creek using gravel with a bamboo brush to scour her blackened rice cauldron. Frogs called at the sound of her scraping, and the woman laughed when Ohasu said that they seemed to be commenting on her efforts.

You're going home then?

I haven't seen my mother in three years.

The woman thought it was unusual for a young woman to travel alone, and Ohasu said that she always felt alone. Even when with others.

Is that the way of it?

I do have one good friend. Her name is Oyuki.

Women should be friends with other women. I myself have a husband, and when I am with him, I feel alone. But then when he's away, I miss him.

I see, said Ohasu.

You are unmarried?

Ohasu nodded. I was raised in a poor village and always used to play by myself when I was a child. Perhaps that is why…

When you were a child, the woman said, rinsing her pot; and she smiled at Ohasu and told her that she seemed a child still. For all your scarlet underskirt.

Ohasu continued on through farmland that became increasingly hilly, and by the third day she had reached the mountains. Evening arrived with heat lightning that crackled above the higher peaks to the north like demented needles stitching the earth to the sky. She watched it from the shelter of an abandoned shrine. A stone obelisk celebrated an ancient cedar that had stood there once, the carved words obscured by lichens. Nothing remained of the tree, not even a scar where its stump had been. No one came anymore with gifts of rice wine or barley cakes; yet Ohasu could still feel the reverence that the great tree had inspired, and she wrote her first travel stanza:

Mountain lightning: in the gaps between the trees, the shapes of absent trees.

She added *the shadows of other trees* beside the final phrase, and sat gazing out at the twilight forest, her writing brush poised, unable to choose between the two ideas and wondering what Old Master Bashō would have said about them.

The evening rain arrived, and Ohasu sat huddled in her bower like a drab bird and nibbled on a cold rice ball, her meagre possessions tucked all around her. I'm not lonely, she said aloud, as if that might make it true.

Ohasu had been in the Nightless City for a few weeks when the man who would eventually become her patron asked to visit her. They tell me you cry yourself to sleep every night, the iris lover had said.

Ohasu had knelt before the old man, slumped and self-conscious, a frightened little girl wearing bright new gaudy-robes much too big for her.

Why do you do that?

She had looked at her hands.

The other new one you have here, what's her name?

Does she do it too?

Oyuki.

Oyuki. Does Oyuki cry at night too?

Sometimes.

Sometimes. But you cry more?

Ohasu had said nothing so the old iris lover had said, What would your mother say if she knew you were crying?

She would cry too.

The old man had laughed. That wouldn't do, would it? The two of you soaking the tatami mats. He had waited for her to smile too then said, Were you always such a baby?

No. She had looked up at him for the first time, her eyes brimming with tears. But for all her fear and uncertainty about what was required of her, this old man had seemed kind; and she'd told him how she had been happy in her village, and how whenever her mother went to wash clothes, she would play on the stream bank and float bamboo-leaf boats on the current. She would decorate them with tiny flowers for cargo and a beetle or two for crew then set them bobbing on the water, trailing along beside them as they swirled and eddied in the ripples and foam. Her mother would watch her games. And soon she too would be making her own flower vessels to launch on the stream, also pleased when one of the frail craft negotiated a difficult cataract, and dismayed if it foundered and the crew was lost.

That was what I liked, Ohasu had said. And I want to go home and do it again.

The old man had listened to her then said, I used to make leaf boats too.

With your mother?

No. By myself. And he'd asked her which kind of bamboo leaves she had found most buoyant, and had she ever tried to contrive a sail?

Ohasu woke early to sunlight, the wet earth steaming as the night's rain returned to the sky to fall again. She ate another rice ball then packed up her carry-sack without bothering to make tea and set out. Her path led downhill into a broad swale of swampy ground, the waterlogged surface filled with duck weed and wild ginger. She planted the last of her rhizomes there then continued on. Dragonflies hovered in the air before her or lit on the tips of tall reeds like sentinels charged with monitoring traffic in the marshlands. Standing water covered the path at low spots; and she waded in with her hems lifted, the fragrant mud yielding as she picked her way forward, dispersing water striders that dimpled the water-surface, more the shadows of creatures than creatures.

The bottom of the boggy land became softer. Ohasu tried to push her way past the low spot, but her sandals were soon trapped. She pulled one free and stepped backward but the other was completely mired. She stood trying to work it loose, feeling the warmth of the suction of the mud. Tiny brown aquatic creatures had arrived to investigate her ankles, transporting themselves on barely visible limbs that seemed to be both feet and fins, and she paused, waiting until they had reached their own conclusions about her presence there, then unwound the rice straw cord of the trapped sandal and tugged it out as she backed onto the firmer mud behind her, pleased with the place and the day.

On leafless branches, crows are settling: autumn twilight.

OHASU FOUND A NIGHT'S LODGING with a widow whose children had all died young. The widow still wept when she recited their names on New Year's Day, listing them in order and counting up what their ages would have become. She knew it was foolish but she did it anyway. Her oldest was a girl who would have been sixteen this year, and Ohasu said that she herself was sixteen.

The woman had thought she seemed younger.

I'm small for my age.

They sat with barley tea on the veranda that looked out over tiered rice fields being drained in preparation for harvest. The fields were not hers, and the widow took little pleasure in them although a small portion of the harvest was always left with her, and she was permitted to glean the cut fields before the stubble was burned. She said she found no satisfaction in her life.

Probably you are unacquainted with what the world asks of women, the widow said; and Ohasu said she thought probably she was acquainted with some of it.

The widow said that every age had its unique requirements. Girls sang about things that made grannies weep. What seemed a novelty to young women became tedious for those older. A girl travelling alone would be burdened by uncertainty while an old woman living alone might look back at such a state with fondness. She said she had long wondered if the death of her last child was worse than the death of the first. She had been told that although each death had its own shape, the incense burned for one child rose for all and was shared among them. She said she had thought that her fourth child, a girl she named Yuri, might survive. She had toddled about with great determination, laughing when she fell and getting up again delighted with herself, as if the pleasure of being upright on her fat little legs was more than worth the occasional tumble. I used to tie her onto my back when I worked in the fields and carry her everywhere with me. She was a baby who seldom cried and soon brightened when she did. The widow told Ohasu she had loved each of her other babies, but the love she felt for Yuri was crueller because hopeful. She had a suck dummy I made for her. It was her only possession. And when she too died and her small body rose in smoke to the sky, I carried that suck dummy with me tucked behind my obi sash and felt it there like a hard knot. Then my last child was born and died so easily that it seemed as if an accordance had been reached with death, with existence being allowed long enough for a name to be attached so that there would be a word available for use during mourning. Then my husband died. In the morning in the sunlight on the veranda with his eyes open. She said it was like a breath that didn't finish itself. Since then for her each day had followed the one before it and always seemed slightly softer, slightly thinner, slightly less available, and what she had had of her family, her memories of them, had also begun to fade. Now I'm waiting for my own death. It seems to me slow in arriving.

Do you have nothing for yourself that you cherish?

What is there for me?

Ohasu didn't know. She gazed out at the darkening fields, hearing the sound of the water draining from upper rice paddies to lower ones in a set of steady trickles, an array of little waterfalls dropping from one level to the next and emptying finally into the channels that led down to the stream. That sound of water, the music of it. How the world in itself is soothing.

But the woman told her that such sentiments only meant she was young still. When she was older she would no longer delude herself.

A pair of chestnut trees marked where the road to Ohasu's village turned off from the main road. They were exactly as they had been. Farther on would be a shallow stream with a fording place built up with stones; it was easy enough to manage in autumn but during the summer floods crossing it could be perilous.

But she arrived to find a new bridge spanning the stream, the support pillars capped with bronze lotus-bud finials, and beside it was a shop offering yam gruel as a famous local product. Ohasu called in at the doorway to ask if what they provided was indeed the true type of yam gruel made there.

A woman sitting beside a rough brown crock filled with bell flowers laughed at the question. What other kind would it be?

Just that in some areas, sugar is used.

Not here, said the shop woman. Although a dribble of sweet rice wine is poured in.

And is *konyaku* also included?

It would not be it without it.

In some places, burdock or carrot is used.

That may be the way elsewhere.

I wonder if *shiitake* is also omitted?

The woman looked at her sharply. You're very concerned with our yam gruel.

It's been over three years since I've tasted the true form of it, Ohasu said, hovering uncertainly. But I can't stop, for my mother doesn't yet know I'm coming home.

She reached her village by the hour of the cock. The sunlight slanted across the fields, filling them with a dusty golden light; and she walked along beside the stream where she had played as a child, the cotton-woods on the far bank still the same, the willows trailing their long branches above the flow as they always did. She saw plants she recognised, rocks that were familiar, and she strode along the path, nodding at the puzzled surprise of villagers who could not quite pull the child out of the young woman before them. There was to be no stopping now, nothing to delay the pleasure of the sight of her mother at her loom, or in the scullery, or in the lean-to shed where they kept their food storage jars.

Her cottage was as it had been. She shoved open the sliding door boldly and called out in a child's voice, Here I am home!

A woman she didn't know looked up at her. She was only a few years older than Ohasu, and she knelt in the middle of the room with her sleeves tied back, stripping soybeans out of their pods.

Is my mama not here? Ohasu asked, as if the years spent in Edo were no more than mist burned off in the morning sun; and the woman observed her for a moment then invited her to come inside. I will tell you about her, she said.

Speaking of things chills the lips: the autumn wind.

HER PATH CURVED AROUND a high alpine meadow then led back into the forest. She found an abandoned shack at the edge of the trees, the roof thatching so overgrown with wild grasses gone to seed that it looked like a tomb-mound, with pads of velvet moss thickening the undersides of the eaves and woody tree ears stacked in scallops on the support posts. She waited outside then went in. The hut had once been occupied by a follower of the way of *haikai* linked poetry, and stanzas written out on strips of rice paper were glued onto an interior wall like an assertion of order in the wilderness. There were gaps where poems had fallen away and been lost, but clusters of three or four consecutive links remained in most areas, and longer runs also still existed.

Geese came sailing in around the rim of the forest. They flapped down awkwardly onto the shelf of dried mud that rimmed the autumn marshlands, commenting on what was to be found there. Ohasu went out to collect pine boughs, and several of the geese paused to observe her at her labours. She arranged the boughs beside the hearth then spread her quilts on them. In her carry-sack was a parcel her father had given her. He had prepared it himself, one of the two things his new wife would not do for him, the other being to tell Ohasu that she could have no home with them.

Ohasu retrieved the little parcel and sat holding it. Her dried umbilicus was packaged within a folded square of white rice paper fastened with a hemp string. She opened the packet, her tears dropping on the flat leathery knot as if the flow of them might soften it. She had also been given a lock of her mother's hair as a keepsake, tied at one end with a bit of silk thread, and a few of the twig dolls she had made as a child that her mother had preserved in her love for her.

Her hair was still black, Ohasu had said; and her father had looked away and said nothing.

There had been no incense to burn at her mother's tomb. Ohasu had gathered together a few sprigs of sweet olive and arranged them there, the tiny yellow flowers inconspicuous within their shiny green leaves but the perfume lush as jasmine.

Her father's new wife had told her she was sorry.

Ohasu had stood in the doorway and looked out at the road and the fields and forests and the mountains beyond, the world as it had been on every day of her childhood, whitened with snow in winter or wreathed in spring mists or shimmering in the heat waves of a summer's day. She had looked back at the cottage from the roadway, and she had looked back at her village from the upper curve of the road that led back into the cedar forest. The one thing she had not been able to do was tell her mother she forgave her for sending her away.

The little twig dolls were dressed in scraps of mulberry paper that she had dyed with the juice of berries. The purple and red of the skirts and jackets had faded and blackened over the months and years, and the paper had become brittle so she fitted the little dolls carefully within the creases of the packet with her umbilicus and the curl of her mother's hair then refolded it carefully, wound it within an extra obi sash, and tucked it away in her carry-sack.

Most of the geese had settled into feeding, but several at the edge of the flock continued their colloquy, addressing matters that must be resolved before they too could relax; and as Ohasu watched them her weeping stopped, and she thought she would not weep again for anything ever.

The following morning she studied the stanzas glued to the inside wall. None was known to her. The calligraphy had the feel of the previous century, a kind of controlled tension that typified the linking poets of the years of chaos before the Tokugawa armies imposed peace. She could tell it had been a classical hundred-stanza effort – the moon stanzas and flower stanzas had survived and were in their appointed places – and she thought she could distinguish the three hands involved, suggesting that each participant had written out his own poems.

She chose an empty space that had once held the link connecting a run of three love stanzas to a splendid one on the moon. What was needed was something like the sadness of lovers parting at dawn. She wiped clean the plaster there then brush-wrote her own stanza directly onto the wall, creating a new transition across the interval and signing 'Ohasu' at the bottom in kana. She added only that one link because she was only one person. Perhaps if others came here they would see what she had done with her gap on the wall and do the same, and the entire sequence would eventually be reconfigured – different from what it had been originally yet still participating in it.

The road continued higher and the air grew cooler even in sunlight. Ohasu had a lined sleeveless over-jacket that she wore even though it was too large for her; but she had brought no heavy cloaks or padded robes, and she knew she would soon need them.

Darkness caught her before she found a lodging for the night. She settled in a small dell screened by cedars. It was the first time she had slept under the night sky, and she stared up at the frozen stars, at the astonishing multiplicity and brilliance of them, the silver river flowing across the sky in the density of its beauty; and she awoke to that same sky fading with the arrival of dawn, so stiff from the cold that she was hardly able to repack her quilts.

She stumbled out onto the road shivering and began walking to warm herself. Dew coated the roadside grasses and smoothed the dust of the road. She reached a high-point as the sun rose and saw beyond it an expanse of forest, mountain after mountain after mountain extending to the rim of the world, the dark green of the cedars and cypresses beneath the pink and gold of the arriving day like the offer of an embrace from the earth to the sky. The sun warmed her as she gazed out at the certainty of the world, and the urge to celebrate what she saw filled her with joy. She had not told her mother she forgave her. But she told her now. And she felt as she did so that even a small person such as herself could live without fear in a world that was a prayer and a validation.

Along this road goes no one: autumn twilight.

OHASU REACHED THE OUTSKIRTS of the northern town of Black Feathers late in the afternoon. The road ran beside the river, with tea houses and noodle shops lining both sides of it as far as the bridge. She shuffled along with her belongings on her back, surveying the town, then returned to the large riverside teahouse at the top end of the road.

A group of pleasure providers had gathered on a raised reed-mat platform erected against the back wall, their sandals left unpaired in a sloppy pile at the base. Bowls of mountain stew were being distributed, accompanied by a tray of pickled radish slices; and they called for Chinese-style tea but received only a pot of boiled barley tea poured from the public kettle.

Ohasu settled at a small table off to the side and watched the women and drum-boys at their meal, chopsticks jabbing like the beaks of starlings, picking out the stringy bits of meat first, as if what they had been given might at any moment be snatched away.

They chewed with concentration, spitting out snarls of gristle only after working it for every shred of nourishment, and Ohasu wondered if she could learn to eat what they ate.

Among the pleasure providers was a woman younger and taller than the others. A punishment brand had been burned into her forehead leaving raised welts, and both her nostrils had been ripped open instead of slit cleanly so that her nose had healed into a spongy mass shot through with inflamed wedges of scarring. She seemed undismayed by her evil fortune and ate with good appetite, leaning forward to spear slices of yellow radish from the shared tray and allowing a single white breast to slide out from the loosely closed bodice of her robe, the mauve bud of the nipple chaffed from the gums of a suckling.

Ohasu was asked what she wanted, and she smiled and thanked the maid and said she was fine as she was.

But what did she want?

Nothing.

You can't have nothing.

Tea then.

Real tea or barley tea?

Ohasu didn't know.

Real tea is three coppers and barley tea is one.

Barley tea then.

One of the drum-boys set aside his empty bowl and took up a samisen, finger-plucking it softly. He seemed to be working out an idea that had just occurred to him; and although his playing was not polished, he was quick to see the possibilities in the line he was extending into the room, twisting out subtle variations for the satisfaction of doing so. It occurred to Ohasu that she did not understand the lives of people in the world, and that although the fault was not hers, failure to correct it would be.

A pair of Dewa samurai had stopped in the doorway. They took the best table at the front; and the house maid carried over a ceramic crock and poured milky liquor into their bowls, releasing a sour fragrance into the air and causing the Dewa men to congratulate each other, pleased with the earliness of the hour, the potency of their tipple, and their prospects for an evening of indulgence.

The young woman with the destroyed face came over to Ohasu. You should try to avoid them, she whispered.

Ohasu glanced at her meekly. They seem rough.

They will soon become rougher. The disfigured woman settled in beside her. It's no concern of ours, but if you're looking for back work, you would be wise to choose another place.

I'm not looking for work of any sort. Ohasu gazed at the damaged woman, as if unwilling to insult her by averting her eyes. I'm a student of linked poetry. I hope to visit the holy mountains of Dewa.

Well, they'll put a girl-poet on her back here soon enough, said the woman. But you're carrying a permission?

Ohasu looked back at her but said nothing.

Even with one, there's little reason to go up there. I don't know about Moon Peak or The Sky Baths, but the temples on Black Feathers Mountain are hard places unfit for any woman.

Ohasu thought about this then said, And is your life here very severe?

I used to think so.

But now it's better?

Now I don't think about it.

The others on the platform stacked their empty bowls on the serving tray then pulled out long bamboo pipes and settled themselves, ready for whatever their evening would bring. The disfigured woman told Ohasu that she had had a husband once, a fisherman who drowned in the sea, leaving her with two small children. The children had both died – first the younger then the elder – and to pay her debts, she had agreed to do back work in the pleasure quarters of Sendai. But after her punishment, she had been deemed unacceptable and had come here. Her new babe was a weak and fretful thing that cried at night, and she had little hope for her.

Have you named her?

I have not. And I won't until there's some indication she might survive.

Ohasu nodded at this then said, Why were you punished?

The woman's lips pressed together then twisted slightly, as if she were trying to work out a bit of sinew caught between two teeth. I was punished for being stupid, she said. I was punished for being available when they came for me. And for not killing my tormentors. For not cutting out their selfish hearts with a sharp knife.

And not severing their man-parts then stuffing them in the holes where their hearts should have been. I was punished for seeking some release from my suffering. Why are any of us punished? It is for such reasons.

Ohasu sat with the woman in the fading autumn twilight and watched as the evening's customers passed by. The rural northern samurai disguised themselves much as did those in the city, either in shame at their poverty or in fear of the latest edicts against unacceptable behaviour. The local merchants strode along flaunting themselves although their robes were less elegant than those worn in Edo, and their sashes were not in the current fashion.

The Dewa bravos had noticed Ohasu and called over to her. She tucked her small face away, and the disfigured woman shouted back that she was a tender child from the south and not charmed by northern manners.

Is that the way of it?

Ohasu remained silent, and the disfigured woman declared that what they wanted would be unknown to her.

Perhaps we can teach her, said one; but their wine was gone, and they called out for more then turned their attention to the fresh crock when it arrived.

I was punished for stealing, the disfigured woman declared softly. But what I took was mine.

Ohasu nodded at this then said, I have what is mine. I am it.

A light breeze rose, and the evening sky held the green and glassy clarity of late autumn. Ohasu spotted a group of happy-day celebrants accompanying a palanquin that bore the commercial crest of a Sendai merchant family. The motley crowd swirling around this conveyance displayed the eager flamboyance of those who have discovered a rich patron with more money than sense. There were moorland drum-boys among them, and rustic contortionists and animal mimics, as well as musicians and tale-singers and stage actors who wore the same robes for every role. Even a monkey beggar had joined in, leading a scabrous old ape that gazed about with frighten eyes and clung to the rope around his neck with scaly black hands.

The disfigured woman had gone to attend to her baby, and Ohasu moved outside as the palanquin with its party of revellers halted in front of the wineshop. The lattice side screen was slid open to reveal the face of a young profligate whose cheeks were flushed with wine. Are you available?

Ohasu nodded shyly.

What can you do? he asked in a voice furred by days and nights of debauchery.

Ohasu hesitated then said, I am a dancer from Edo.

From Edo? You know any of the new dances?

Many of them, Ohasu said.

The most popular ones?

Most of them.

The dissolute youth stared at Ohasu for a long moment, then his eyes lost focus and he was staring past her. I pay twenty coppers for the night, he said and slid shut the lattice screen. Ohasu took up her carry-sack and fell in with the party of entertainers.

A drum-boy sidled up to her. How much did he tell you? The boy had smeared his face with white makeup to conceal the pustules that crusted his lips and eyelids.

Twenty coppers.

For the night?

Yes.

The boy pondered this. He said all will be paid the same. But they often forget, and favour some over others. His tongue darted out and toured his infected lips. What are you? A dancer?

Ohasu bowed in quick acknowledgement.

Do you dance 'naked islanders' style?

No. Wearing my gaudy robe. In the manner of the kabuki dramas.

A knotted sash, are you? The boy smirked at her. Then you won't last long with us. Our patron is a connoisseur of the small hole. And he chooses to indulge himself.

Their destination was an assignations teahouse at the far end of the town, and their route took them past the entry-plaza to the river bridge. Beyond the bridge lay the steep road leading up into the first of the holy mountains of Dewa, and Ohasu slowed her pace as they passed it then abruptly turned away and hurried up onto the arched wooden structure itself.

One of the guards intercepted her before she had reached mid-span. A large, circular Tokugawa crest was painted on the centre of his breastplate and a smaller one decorated his red-lacquer flat helmet. Ohasu admitted she had no permission to pass. She told him that she was a small and unimportant person.

It was her desire to make a pilgrimage to the shrines and temples on the holy mountains of Dewa and pray for the repose of the soul of the man who had been her benefactor.

Was he a Dewa man? asked the guard.

Ohasu admitted that he was not.

Then there can be no reason for you to go up there.

There is no reason for me to be anywhere, Ohasu told him. She said she was like a withered seed-pod blowing across the surface of the earth, with no vitality or necessity.

Then there's also no reason for you to abandon your companions, said the guard.

Ohasu watched the party of celebrants as they began filing into the assignations teahouse, their raucous cries like those of birds tossed in an autumn gale; then instead of following them, she turned away and started walking back in the direction she had come from.

The Road to Black Feathers
黒 羽 の 道

The boy came ambling across the autumn moorlands, clouds of insects rising up around him in the slanting orange light of the late afternoon sun. He wore a crazy-style robe of mismatched panels, and his two swords were shoved together through his sash in such a manner that the fist-protector of one would probably impede access to the other. On his head was the kind of iron helmet no fighter would employ unless facing imminent battle, a riveted old brain-roaster that resembled the petrified carapace of a tortoise, the chin cords dangling disreputably, the metal plates on the neck guards collecting dust and debris, and the rusty stub of a snapped-off flange on the frontal plate indicating where some form of heraldic device had once been mounted.

Hasegawa Torakage watched the rider's approach from the shade of the eaves of a roadside inn. Travel gear piled behind the boy's saddle was tied on haphazardly with rice-straw ropes as if his provisioning had been organised by apes, and a long wooden pannier hung down awkwardly on one side, unbalancing the load so that his horse moved with an oblique and staggering gait. The boy rode past the rogue samurai without so much as a glance and turned up onto the road north.

Hasegawa ordered another flask of the local wine. So how far you going? the innkeeper inquired; and Hasegawa said he hadn't quite decided that yet.

So I guess you'll know when you get there.

I guess so.

Hasegawa finished his wine flask then wrote out a poem card and tacked it on the inn's alcove post:

Ill while travelling, in my dreams still wandering over withered fields.

You said that's by somebody you know?

Used to know. He counted out what he owed, placing the coins one by one in a row on the table. A man who died.

There were places where the road north to Black Feathers was little more than a dyke-path separating two paddy fields, and Hasegawa strode through the yellow-dry sea of rice shimmering in the afternoon light, seeing things remembered from his childhood and things unknown to it.

The road curved up into the deep shade of a cedar forest. An orange bird-perch gate marked a flight of stone stairs climbing straight up to where a cloud-road shrine would be; and a few pilgrims dressed in white were resting there, vows written in bold characters down the fronts of their robes. Hasegawa exchanged greetings with them and comments on the weather and the topography and the pleasures of mountain rambling in high autumn but didn't linger, for they would be a slow-moving company prone to breaking out into prayer chants at the slightest provocation.

Hasegawa reached the next village just before sunset. The foolish boy-warrior was sprawled like a proprietor on the stack of rice-straw sacks that local farmers had prepared for the harvest. You want it? the boy called. His horse stood with its rear hoof held off at an odd angle, the fetlock swollen and bloody. Save me the bother of killing the stupid thing.

You kill it you'll be carrying your gear.

I guess I'll find a replacement first.

You see many horses around here?

The boy shifted his sword handles forward suggestively. I guess I only need one.

Hasegawa looked at him then continued through the village and back onto the mountain road. He walked as far as the ruins of a local daimyo's fortress that had been destroyed by the Tokugawa Shogunate. On the grassy ridge above it was an immense ginkgo tree standing against the sky like a geyser of sulphur-yellow flames. The defenders had been given an opportunity to record their feelings and attach messages and poems and admonitions for their heirs, and these documents had been attached to their head caskets for the trip back to Edo where the shogun himself had agreed to participate in a formal viewing. Nothing was left of the buildings that had been there. Rectangular sections of granite foundation blocks were all that remained, like abandoned jetties washed by a sea of autumn grasses.

Hasegawa built a small comfort-fire on the leeward side of a foundation wall, soot from his smoke blackening that already there; and he sat facing the splendid ginkgo tree that was blazing against the water-bright clarity of the autumn evening sky, recalling phrases from old poems and new ideas of his own. The garrison that had died here were men like himself, men who would have sought consolation in the arranging of words and who had perhaps included a description of that tree even as they were waiting to be called out for the commencement of slaughter procedures...

Shit. I thought you were a bandit. The gaudy boy-warrior came up off the road, his helmet worn so low over his eyes that he had to tilt his head back to see. I was about to get out my old throat-cutter.

The boy was on foot now and leading his horse, the gear as ineptly arranged as before, with rice-straw ropes wound around hither and thither in a comedy of incapability. He declared that he was known every-where as Tarō, the Hell-kite of Edo, and that all men who met him soon realised he was a stone-cold killer with an icy heart and a fondness for the beauty of war.

The boy waited uncertainly at the edge of the camp site, acknowledging Hasegawa's right of priority. Of course I guess we're both up here for the same reason, he said.

I guess I don't know what that could be.

The boy smirked, as if undergoing some obscure hazing ritual. Killing bandits.

Hasegawa watched him but said nothing.

The Hell-kite of Edo seemed to detect no rebuke in the rogue samurai's silence. Of course I haven't had much luck killing any yet. But I'm getting closer. He stood waiting so Hasegawa invited him to bivouac there and share his meagre rations. Unless you prefer to be on your own.

Usually I do, said the Hell-kite. It makes me more deadly.

The lone wolf.

The lone wolf all alone on its own and that strikes like sudden lightning!

All right.

But since you've already got a fire going...

After they had finished their meal, the Hell-kite of Edo retrieved his elongated pannier and placed it on the foundation stone beside the fire. The box was hinged along one side and held closed by a pair of brass hook-and-eye latches on the other. Words written in the language of butter eaters decorated the lid of this foreign box, and inside was a new-design harquebus, a weapon only just arrived in their country and one said to possess a deadly accuracy. The gun had a long barrel with a single-leg shooting support that fitted into a brass socket midway down the length of it. The ramrod rode in a tube on the wooden stock under the barrel, with extra ramrods inside the lid of the box. The Hell-kite said there was no object anywhere in the world that he preferred to this wonderful new gun. A row of sealed canisters contained black powder, and a pair of small metal flasks held the fine-grain priming powder. There was a leather case with adjustable straps for carrying lead balls, and a jute sack filled with little squares of silk that were used to hold the ball in place. The Hell-kite told him he would not trade his gun for a golden Buddha statue big as a man. The weapon was already fitted with its punk cord, and extra cords were coiled up and tucked inside the carrying box along with the tools needed for proper maintenance.

I can kill anything with it I can see, said the Hell-kite. He lifted the matchlock out of its case and cradled it on his lap then held up a lead ball the size of a sparrow's egg. You can imagine the damage that does.

Hasegawa said nothing. But he could imagine it.

The Hell-kite demonstrated how a brass cover closed down over the touch hole so the priming powder wouldn't spill out. I am particularly fond of the art of the way of the head-shot. The punk cord was slotted into a serpentine-lever that cocked back against a spring and was held there by the toggle bar of the trigger release mechanism. He's standing there in the folly of his arrogance. Then, bam! Lightning strikes! And his brains are splattered all over the rocks and trees!

All right.

Or he's on his knees weeping and pleading for his life but you just –

I said all right. Put it back in its box. And don't show me again.

SO HOW MANY MEN have you killed?

Hasegawa looked back at the grinning boy stumping along behind him but said nothing.

More than a hundred?

They were keeping to a ridge, seeking terrain that would be easier for the boy's horse to manage. Hasegawa had squared up his load better, but he was favouring his hind leg.

More than fifty then?

That's no kind of question.

Seems to me it's the only one there is.

Hasegawa said nothing.

I haven't actually killed anybody myself yet. At least I don't think I have.

You'd know.

Not with my big banger you don't!

Hasegawa glanced back at him again.

I needed to get a feel for it. You know how you need to get a feel for a thing like that? It's all very well shooting at trees. Or dogs. Except of course for how they run around so you have to tie them to something so if you miss the first time you can keep trying. But that's not the same as shooting at a man. And you know you want to know you can trust your weapon in battle. So when I got into the hills, there was this gang of ruffians camped on the far side of this deep gorge. Troublemakers of the worst sort probably. So I worked my way around until I found a good spot and let it off on them. What a noise! Echoes in all directions!

And you hit one?

Probably.

You don't know?

Well, no. I had to duck down so they couldn't see where the shot came from.

They stayed just under the ridge line throughout the middle part of the day, climbing higher occasionally to avoid steep inclines. The shogunate constabulary had set up an outpost farther along on the road so when-ever they reached an opening in the forest they would search for the pale wisp of smoke from the day-fire there and estimate their position by it.

You know probably we could have just stayed on the road and gone straight through.

Not with that gun.

That's why it's in its box. So you don't know what it is.

What else would be in a box like that?

They came to an exposed slope of loose scree that descended steeply to a stream far below. The open sky was a hard flat blue with low clouds crowding the ho-rizon, and the mountains and forests stretched out be-yond them endlessly in all directions, dark green on lighter green paling to grey. A sea eagle hung high in the autumn sky, adjusting itself with casual ease as it slid across great lambent sheets of empty air.

The Hell-kite stood watching it with him. What you do is you wait until it lands on its nest then shoot straight up through it.

They went down along the edge of the forest for the better footing that might be found there, and traversed back and forth until they reached the bottom. Summer flooding had eroded the stream banks, and there was no good way to cross. Hasegawa insisted on unloading the horse and carrying the gear separately. He led the horse down through the raw gully, gauging the angle of the slope; but he was unable to keep the animal from stumbling in a panic as the loose gravel broke up be-neath him, and the horse crashed into the stream and fell sideways then staggered upright. Hasegawa got him on solid ground and calmed him. The Hell-kite began piling the gear on again. Hasegawa waited until he was finished then made him take it apart and do it right.

They were too low to see the constabulary men's smoke now, and they had nothing to guide by other than sunlight filtering down through the trees so they cut straight across, trying to hold to an eastern line, until they reached the road north again, well beyond the shogunate outpost.

We should have stayed on this road the whole time. And if anybody said anything about my gun, we'd have just cut them down.

I thought your intention was to kill bandits.

I won't let anybody stop me.

Not even the Tokugawa?

The Hell-kite brushed off his helmet and put it on, the formality of road travel requiring such a display. I guess they piss the same colour we do. The neck guards attached around the bottom rim of his head-bucket bothered him, and he tried to angle the crown of it forward so the hanging iron strips wouldn't chafe his shoulders. You can take them off, Hasegawa said; they unhook. But the boy thought they gave him a fierce appearance, and that was an advantage he would not willingly forgo.

They bivouacked at the top end of an alpine meadow. They gathered wood and ate their meagre rations beside a scrappy bonfire, the evening wind bending the dry grass and soughing in the tops of the cedars.

The Hell-kite wanted to talk about technique. He said he had a sense of how to fight with a long sword but wasn't sure if his style looked right. What he needed to know was the method of delivering a killing blow. He showed him what he meant, carving great sloppy arcs in the air with his naked blade and delighted by the display until Hasegawa told him he looked like a drunken farmer swinging a grain-flail.

So what should I do then? said the Hell-kite. Give me a few tips.

Tips.

They always say how there's a true way but never say what it is! They always say that the superior man acts without effort but not how he does it. How are you supposed to know?

Hasegawa fed sticks into the fire, watching the flames as they jerked and flared. It's not chopping. It's slicing. And it's not hitting hard, it's drawing the cutting edge smoothly through the target. He adjusted the architecture of his fire, configuring loosely piled ricks that would burn better. And it's not just how quick you are, it's where you start your stroke from. And not the angle you use, but what your opponent thinks you're going to use. And where he is when he recognises his error. And what he can do about it.

But so then how do you know how to do all that?

You don't need to know. No one does.

But what about me? What if I'm attacked? I can get off one shot with my big banger, but it takes time to reload. I need to know how to fight with a long sword and a short sword. And a slash knife.

Don't get attacked.

Easy for you to say.

Hasegawa poked the fire, sending a spray of orange sparks up into the autumn evening.

The Hell-kite told him he knew he made mistakes. But he'd never had any help. How could he follow the true way if nobody guided him? He said he'd rather leave his bones on a hillside than spend his life squatting in some miserable hovel tapping on copper kettles or fitting tufts of bristles onto bamboo handles. That's no life! You think that's a life? Year after year after year of it. Assembling tray stands and gluing the parts together. Your shoulders hunched and your fingers so crooked you can hardly use them! Dipping flax wicks into bubbling pots of wax. Your eyesight failing. Your whole life just that one thing and then you die? Is that a life for a man? He said he'd rather be cut down with a sword in his hand and the sounds of battle in his ears. The shouts of attackers! The roar of musket fire! The howls of the wounded! The stench of blood and the shared beauty of comradeship as you launch a massed charge, every man willing to die for the nobility of the attempt.

What attempt?

What do you mean what attempt?

Attempting what?

Any attempt! he cried. The goal of it hardly mattered to him. It was the willingness to die for something worth dying for that the Hell-kite craved. He couldn't find words strong enough. Just the pure *beauty* of it, he said.

Of men dying...

Of men dying, yes! The beauty of the pathos of their deaths.

You've never seen it.

That's why I'm here! Why do you think I'm up here? Stuck in these stupid mountains? The Shogun's Great Peace meant that for someone like the Hell-kite of Edo, there was no longer any chance for a real war. Either you join up with the bandits or you go fight them, he said.

Hasegawa stared into the tossing fire, the incandescence of it blooming and flaring in the raw mountain wind, the flames ripped apart at the instant of their inception. So all you want is to kill somebody.

The Hell-kite sat stubbornly beside him. You haven't listened to me. I want to do it *properly*. I want to do it the way the men of the past did it. In battle. With the correct technique. For the beauty of the strokes and the nobility of the achievement.

It's just dead people lying on the ground.

That's right! It's all very tragic. Which is why I want to do it the way it's always been done.

Hasegawa found a place to spread his quilts and laid them out with his carry-sack for a pillow. He walked back into the bushes to piss then returned to the edge of the firelight. You can want whatever you want, he said. But you won't get it from me.

THEY PARTED THE NEXT DAY. There wasn't much said. The Hell-kite sat by the morning fire with an extra robe draped over his head.

Hasegawa collected his gear. You know you're going to have to be careful with that horse.

The boy looked up at him sullenly. His horse was his property and of no concern to another man. The stupid thing would just have to get used to its load. If it didn't, it could lie down and die. And good riddance.

The sky was low and heavy with clouds. Hasegawa followed a back road that would lead over the central massif and directly into the holy mountains of Black Feathers. The wind felt colder as he went higher, and the road was overgrown with brush in places and blocked with trees that had fallen, some with long black burn-scars ripped down through their hearts and some rotted-out at the roots and toppled from the weight of their years. He climbed then rested then climbed again. Rime whitened the shadows of the rocks and tree boles, and his breath plumed out whitely before him. It could snow, it was cold enough.

By midday he had emerged into a high-pass of bare rock and scrub pine. The morning's clouds rode in tight piles on the horizon, releasing an empty sky of a blueness of an intensity that seemed beyond praise. He worked his way up around granite outcroppings darkened in places where streams of snow-melt flowed in spring, the broad gray sheets of rock scoured by the wind as if in preparation for an encounter with the sky. He stopped to rest, settling into a protected pocket, the granite there crumbled into a dressing of coarse sand. He scraped up a handful then let it trickle through his fingers, flakes of mica glinting like tiny black blades in the windy sunlight. Everything was provided. You just had to be able to acknowledge it. Lichens encrusted the rock, fitting themselves to its welts and knobs and fissures, mustard yellow or milky grey or the grainy brown of raw burdock, a beauty equivalent in every way to that of cherry blossoms or maple leaves, only smaller, drier, less insistent...

Except they weren't *like* blossoms, they weren't like anything.

Why did the facts of the world seem to him so unfinished?

Why was he still draping the world with words? Still seeing it through them?

Why even when he tried to get past this yearning to describe what he saw did he find himself trying to describe the impossibility of description?

A lichen on a rock in the mountains. Why was it as it is so beyond him?

Hasegawa walked until twilight then set his bivouac in a protected gorge shielded from the wind. A single rice ball wrapped in dried laver was all that remained of his rations, and he tried to feel satisfied but wanted another. He would have no food tomorrow and probably none the following day.

It began snowing at twilight, soft and silent; and he pulled his gear back under a low juniper then cut extra branches and inserted them into the canopy of boughs above him. He sat beside an underfed fire draped in every garment and quilt he possessed, the night's cold sinking into him; and he awoke to white ash where his fire had been, the whiteness of snow covering the high peaks, and a cold so crushing that it drove him numbed and stumbling out onto a frost-covered rock plain where he marched in self-configured circles, his teeth chattering, flapping his arms, trying to get himself warm enough to be able to start another fire.

The bleak sun rose into the milky cold of the sky and the wind rose with it, blowing snow dust off stone peaks in great sweeping bursts of silver that glittered then faded against the whiteness of the dawn. He went scrambling for more wood, anything that would burn, the bitter cold like shafts of ice that drove him staggering back with what he had scavenged. The fire he managed to construct was a poor affair, the wood too green to burn well, and he soon abandoned it, packing up his gear with hands crimped by the cold.

The day warmed as Hasegawa walked but he was never warm. His feet felt like things wrapped in quilts. By the hour of the ram, he had reached an open slope from where he could see the snowy peaks of the three holy mountains in the distance. He left the path and crossed down into a high alpine meadow, the dead grass lying flattened and matted on the frozen earth. Runoff had pooled in low places, the black water edged with a silver filigree of rime; and he was in amidst them when he realised that what he was seeing were human bones scattered across the empty ground, pelvises and femurs and rib cages arrayed like barbaric musical instruments stripped clean by blown grit, as if the cleansing of death's bounty were the true work of the world's wind. There were primitive sword blades here and there, stubby chunks of steel so eaten with rust that they looked like plant fronds or flattened wands of petrified mud. He found the remains of ancient spears, the wooden shafts of which had long since rotted away leaving behind lumps of iron with empty shaft-sockets. Shards of corroded armour sometimes still cupped the bones of its wearer; scraps of cloth broke apart in his fingers and blew away as dust. He found a spray of arrowheads rusted together into a single clump configured by the shape of the arrow canister while the bamboo shafts, the hawks-feather fletchings, the quiver and asymmetrical bow had all long since been absorbed within the sun and the wind and the rain, as had been the bowman himself, whose arrows had not been shot.

A slab of granite held the skulls of the slain piled up neatly in a cairn, their empty eye sockets all facing north towards the holy mountains, as if the orderliness of the arrangement justified the suitability of its occurrence. As if that was all they knew, all you could know. With nothing else to say and nothing to hear said.

THE BANDIT WAS JUST OFF the road, sitting exposed in an open dell. He had both arms wrapped around his belly and his feet sticking straight out before him like a child. A back frame lay abandoned on the roadway, piled high with bundles of dried tobacco leaves, some of which had spilled off, perhaps as a decoy.

The Hell-kite attached the bullet pouch and priming-power flask to his sash then hooked on a pair of black powder canisters. He stuffed a handful of charge-patches in one sleeve pouch the way he'd seen a shogunate gunner do and hid a slash knife in the other except the weight of the stupid thing swinging there annoyed him so he took it out again.

He hiked up through the forest, intending to circle around behind the bandit's defensive position but got lost. The slopes and gullies and outcroppings of rock all looked the same, and what seemed like an easy route would veer off unexpectedly or follow a gentle gradient only to end in the dead-drop of a ravine. He backtracked then tried another route but soon lost patience and went crashing through masses of prickle-brush and groves of willows and alders, kicking and slashing at entangling branches until he blundered out into the open.

The bandit was just downhill, facing away from him. The Hell-kite dropped to his hands and knees then scuttled backwards until he reached an outcropping of rock, his heart pounding. He peeked out over the rock parapet. The bandit hadn't moved. He seemed to have vomited recently, and the front of his robe was splattered with it. The Hell-kite decided it was time for martial greatness. He blew on the punk cord until the tip glowed orange then locked the serpentine-lever back at the fully-cocked safety position. He poured in a charge of black powder. He fitted a lead ball on its patch and drove it home. He primed the pan at the touch hole then closed the pan-cover, humming a wavering little farrago of war ballads under his breath as he shortened the serpentine to half-cock then rested the long barrel of his harquebus against the flanks of the rock.

The bandit disappeared in the smoke of the discharge, the roar of it echoing in the autumn hills. The Hell-kite ducked down behind his rock cover. Even distant enemies would have heard that shot and known what it meant; and the Hell-kite felt overwhelmed by injustice. He was always obliged to do everything on his own and with no help from anyone ever. But when he finally dared to look up again, he saw the bandit lying on his back, a flap of meat knocked out of his shoulder and his legs kicking in an odd manner. He thought he'd have time to get off another shot before reinforcements launched a counterattack.

The Hell-kite opened his bullet pouch and picked out a lead ball, the sounds of battle thudding in his ears, horses charging and men shouting their war cries as the famous bandit-queller seated the ball in a patch of silk cloth and fitted it in the muzzle then drew the ramrod and drove it down smartly into the firing breech, pleased with his skill and his calmness and his panache.

Except he had forgotten to put in the powder charge first.

He squatted back down behind the rocky outcrop at his primary shooting position and felt his eyes fill with tears of rage as he cursed his fate, cursed the sun and the moon and the stars in the sky. Why did everything always have to happen to him?

The Hell-kite had a tool that could be used to force loose a blockage in the gun breech but he hadn't brought it with him. He sat and gathered his thoughts. Then he turned the harquebus upside down and began slamming and banging the muzzle on the hard surface of granite, battering it harder and harder until the stupid ball was jarred loose and dropped into the dirt.

The bandit had come upright on his knees. One arm hung dangling, but he had some kind of vicious-looking knife in his good hand with a blade the colour and shape of a dried wisteria pod.

The Hell-kite pulled the stopper out of his black powder canister with trembling hands and dropped it. He poured in a charge then looked around for the stopper. He couldn't find it so he tucked the still-open canister in a rock-cleft where it wouldn't spill. He picked up the lead bullet and wiped it off then fitted it on a fresh patch and drove it home. The missing stopper had been under his foot. He snatched it up then stood holding the charged gun in one hand, the stopper in the other, staring down at the black power canister, unsure which to put down and which to pick up, his panic growing so that he tossed away the stopper and primed his gun, a loose spray of fine-grain powder spilling down his arm.

The bandit had managed to get to his feet. He was bent over at the waist but still carrying his sword.

The Hell-kite closed the pan-cover then eased the serpentine forward to half-cock. The bandit had spotted him and started up towards his battlements.

The blast tore across the Hell-kite and he threw himself away from it, screeching and rubbing his burned arm, trying to slap away the pain.

But his enemy was on his back again, writhing like a gaffed eel, the lower portion of his face shot away.

The Hell-kite watched as the bandit rolled over onto his belly. He started dragging himself towards the sanctuary of a grove of alders, his shattered arm flopping loosely beside him, a flap of bloody flesh hanging where his cheek had been, his smashed jaw canting out from the side of his head like a poorly-fit handle.

This time he said it aloud: charge first then patched bullet. This time when he spilled priming powder he brushed it away before storming the enemy fortifications. He was determined to conduct himself in the manner of an established bandit-killer killing bandits. He hadn't brought his barrel-support and so was required to hand-hold the heavy gun, and his next bullet only tore a furrow across the bandit's buttocks, jerking him around so that he presented his ruined face back towards his assailant, his cheek ripped open, the edge of raw bone from his jaw hung with a wobbly snarl of bloody meat.

The Hell-kite prepared to reload again. But he'd stupidly left the canister of black powder at his primary assault position. He went scrambling back for it, keening in frustration at the unfairness of things and only remembering once he got there that a second canister was attached to his sash. He calmed himself. Now was a time for skill and resolve and tactical cunning. And panache. He reloaded again calmly, carefully, and returned to the battlefield. He confirmed that his enemy had not regained sufficient mobility to regroup his forces then found a good place to sit with the gun supported on his knees and shot him again, blowing a bright splash of blood out of his neck.

The bandit rolled over onto his back, bleeding into the dust from all parts of him.

With the tide of battle turned in his favour, the Hell-kite of Edo decided to confront his enemy in hand-to-hand combat. He seized him by one foot and dragged him more out into the open, twisting him over onto his belly in the process. The bandit probably couldn't retrieve his sword; but the Hell-kite was cautious by nature, and he kicked the thing farther away then drew his own long sword, revered symbol of the warrior's soul. This was what it was like. He darted forward, slashing down hard as he did so and employing what he understood to be the deadly 'oblique-style' technique of a skilled neck-cutter. But he'd swung too soon, his aim was poor, and his sword tip only took off an ear as it crashed into the side of the already mutilated jaw, ripping it apart in a spray of blood slobber and broken teeth.

The Hell-kite paused and gathered himself. He was too excited. This was his opportunity to become what he wished to be, and he wanted to remember it. But he also had to hurry before the stupid bandit bled to death.

He moved around to where he would have a better angle and swung a mighty swing, hitting him too high again, opening another deep gash on his head and driving his face into the dirt.

The bandit lay prostrate with blood leaking out of his broken-open mouth, bits of bone and teeth jammed up into odd quadrants of what was left of his face so that the Hell-kite panicked and hit him again in fury and disappointment and despair at the unfairness of things, this blow too glancing off the bandit's skull; and he started hacking downwards wildly with blow after blow, cracking into his neck with some strokes and ricocheting off his skull with others, gouts of blood splashing up and bits of meat flying, finally managing to chop the head free so that he could kick it away in triumph.

He stood over him panting, the scourge of bandits, the implacable restorer of justice and stern provider of retribution for all the suffering inflicted on all the ... sufferers.

The Hell-kite pulled off the dead man's robe and spread it on the ground then rolled the head onto it with his foot and tied up the sleeves to form a carry-sack. It was a poor thing, he knew, with most of the features hacked away; but there would come a time when he would look back over a distinguished career of saving towns and villages from the depredations of bandits, and remember this first moment of courage and daring, and smile ruefully and nod modestly and forgive himself for its awkwardness and accept the praise of those who owed him so much and to whom he had become something of a legend and a wonder and a marvel.

He felt a sudden urge to urinate and thought he might do it on the corpse of his opponent but was also a little frightened by that idea and so pissed instead on the bandit's hidden fortress, the yellow of his urine bubbling amidst the green of the alder bushes.

There were no villagers nearby to appreciate the service he had done for them so the Hell-kite started back to his pre-battle camp, intending to hide his gear then continue on to Black Feathers with his trophy for the pleasure of the praise he would find there. He lost his way once but then spotted a familiar gorge and headed off again in the right direction.

Then he stopped as if maul-struck. He had forgotten his harquebus on the battlefield.

His head dropped, and he almost wept at this latest demonstration of the injustice that dogged him so that even now, in his moment of victory, he still had to compensate for the stupid karma that had caused him to be born the child of peasant instead of the son of a samurai. Nothing came easily for him. Nothing was ever given to him. He was on his own always and had to do everything himself, with no help from anybody ever.

The Hell-kite got back to his camp late in the afternoon. His horse lay on its side shivering. When it spotted him approaching, the horse began struggling to get up. But its damaged leg would no longer support it, and it toppled over each time and screamed in a sound he hadn't known could be made by a horse.

The world hated him and mocked him and never helped him; and the Hell-kite darted in and stabbed the stupid horse in the belly, barely avoiding its flailing legs, then stabbed it again and jumped back and watched as it began dying.

The Hell-kite dragged his gear around to a low, marshy dell and hid it in a grove of willows there. It was too late to reach Black Feathers. Warriors lived off the land, and he thought he could butcher the horse although he was unsure how to go about it. He took his small sword – his long sword, the warrior's soul, was too precious for such menial tasks – and started sawing at the horse's haunch. It was harder to cut than he would have thought. His neglecting the edges of his blades might have been partially at fault. But nobody ever showed how to care for them; and he began jabbing at the tough hide, slashing and hacking in his rage and frustration until he had managed to gouge a ragged crater into the flanks of the dead animal, earning a few strips of stringy meat for his troubles.

He built a fire pit with rocks then started his evening fire. He regretted not having a more martial battle-camp, with watch fires blazing on the horizon, and war banners mounted on tall poles. He wished he had an enclosure with camp stools and a rack for displaying the heads of slain warriors. He would have liked to sit up under the full moon after the others had retired and gaze on the heads of the men he had overcome in battle and speculate on the sadness of the nature of things. Or perhaps just the sliver of a three-day moon in a clear sky? Or, no, the full-moon but wreathed in mist. And the cries of fearful prisoners pleading to be spared. And maybe their wives and daughters on their knees begging for mercy. And the melancholy note of a single flute mournfully tootling of the sadness of things. So then not the cries of captives but just a row of severed heads in the moonlight. But still maybe a few daughters, young ones with long lustrous hair. And also only wearing their underskirts. And how at first they're afraid of him but then when he's in his quilts they all creep in too. Or maybe just one does. But then on the next night a different one.

When the fire seemed about right he washed the horse meat in the nearby stream then skewered it on peeled willow sticks. He raked apart the fire to expose a bed of glowing coals then positioned the strips of stringy meat between two upright stones. He went off to collect more firewood and returned to find that the skewers had burned through in the centre before the meat was hardly more than singed, and his meal had dropped onto the fire, smothering the flames so that he had to pluck out the raw chunks of muscle and take them down to the stream to rinse off again then come back and get his fire blazing again, almost incapacitated with frustration.

He sat holding the raw meat staring at nothing as he waited for his fire to grow back then banked the burning branches under the tallest upright wedge of granite and draped the stringy bits of muscle down over the front of it. The bottoms charred while the tops of each strip remained raw, but by reversing them and moving them around this way and that, he managed to burn the flesh sufficiently to be able to choke it down. War drums wouldn't have helped.

That night the Hell-kite of Edo awoke with a searing pain in his belly. He thought he'd been stabbed, and he staggered up out of his quilts on his hands and knees and vomited in great heaving gasps then blundered stumbling down to the stream and fell to his knees at the edge of it, clenching himself in his misery and rage at the world that never relented, never relaxed in its determination to humiliate him. He drank deeply then started back up towards his quilts, and an abrupt spasm in his bowels suddenly flooded him open in an uncontrollable rupture so that he barely squatted in time, jerking his robes up as he emptied himself, the stench of it awful, splattering his heels and ankles in this final violation of his dignity and panache.

THE FOLLOWING DAY, exhausted, starving, bent with cramps, the Hell-kite of Edo shoved his swords through his sash and set out on the road that he thought would take him into the hamlet of Black Feathers, his harque-bus wrapped in a light quilt and the bandit's head in its robe blackened and filthy with dirt and dried blood.

The morning sun burned just above the ridge line of the high mountains surrounding him, and he walked with an ache in his belly that would not cease. He found what he thought might be blackberries and tasted them but only vomited again, hacking up a thin, watery bile. He drank from creeks he passed, having forgotten his water gourd at his bivouac site, and he stopped occasionally and sat in flecks of sunlight and stared at the empty blue sky.

He walked throughout the morning and into mid-day. By the hour of the ram, he had reached a narrow valley that was thick with flowering pampas grasses, the silver filaments of their seed feathers glowing in the late autumn sunlight. The path he was following led straight through this dry moorlands as if it had been cut with a blade. There was no stream that he could see, but an outcropping of rock bordered the path, and he flopped down to rest, his long gun beside him.

His eyes closed in the warmth of the autumn sun, the sound of the wind in the trees and the smell of the dust of the earth, and he dozed off then jerked awake.

He stared up at the grossly huge man observing him from the road. He was wearing old-style body armour of polished leather strips that were the pink and purple of raw flesh and laced with red silk cords. His immense badger-belly protruded like a great flabby drum, and his too-large coiffure was so heavily oiled that it left a greasy patina to the rolls of fat on the back of his neck. The huge man's arms and shoulders and fleshy red face bore the traces of healed slash wounds and contusions, and he leaned on his heavy cudgel and gazed down at the sick boy.

You're carrying something with you, Jirobei said.

No concern of yours, said the Hell-kite.

The huge man looked up at the steeply vertical mountains arranged all around them, the highest peaks already white with snow. You don't belong here.

I'm called Tarō, Hell-kite of Edo, harvester of bandits.

Very good.

No one disputes my ferocity.

I'm sure that is the case.

The huge man sat down across from him, his massive buttocks resting directly on the dirt. What's your family name?

Family name?

Jirobei nodded at the two sword hilts protruding from the boy's obi sash. Your samurai name.

Tarō of Edo is what I use.

Jirobei said nothing.

The boy waited then said, Is this the road to Black Feathers?

Is that where you wish to go?

I have been in these mountains for weeks, fighting bandits. I need rest. I need food and wine and warm quilts to sleep on.

Jirobei's eyes on him didn't waver. What are you carrying?

The boy pulled the harquebus up onto his lap in a demonstration of ownership; but Jirobei held his hand extended with the fat red palm turned upwards, thick as a saddle. Show me.

It's mine, said the boy, but he handed him the gun.

That too.

He picked up the bundle and gave it to him.

Jirobei examined the harquebus then put it aside. He unfolded the blood-stiffened robe until the mangled head was exposed, hacked with slash marks, bits missing, a shard of half-jaw wrenched out sideways, the whole of it clotted and foul. You're supposed to wash it. You wash it then comb out the hair and oil it then configure the topknot again with a pure white-paper tie and attach a name tag to it. You mount it on a shelf-stand and scent it with incense. Or, if you require it for activities at a later date, you place it in a cask of rice wine as a preservative and attach the name tag to the cask handle.

I didn't have time to do any of that.

Jirobei said nothing.

Who would do all that?

Samurai do that for the men they kill, Jirobei said, his eyes like two frozen stones buried behind fat red slabs of flesh. I myself don't.

So I guess that means you aren't samurai. I guess I didn't need to be told that.

That is what it means. He placed the mangled head beside the harquebus. Give me your long sword.

Never, said the boy.

Give it to me.

Why do you want it?

Give it to me.

The boy stared at him and waited then said, What will happen if I do?

What will happen is already determined. Whatever occurs here was always meant to occur here. It's correct as it is in itself. You walked to it, and I walked to it. It fits itself, neither too long nor too short, neither too heavy nor too light. It is perfect in the shape and heft of its instant. How could it ever be otherwise? Can you even conceive of an event that fails to conform to the expectations of itself? Of course you can't. The idea is impossible. From the day you were born, you were coming here to me. You must understand this in order to find your own place in the web of things. The sword wants the transfer. Hand it to me.

I can't...

You can't?

The boy shook his head, his lower lip quivering and his eyes filling with tears. I'm afraid.

You're afraid. All right. Jirobei observed him mildly then reached over and lifted the sword away, the suddenness of it such that the boy's mouth dropped open in surprise.

He drew the blade out halfway and observed the

dullness of the skin of the steel, the traces of discolour-ing that would soon become rust. He drew it out all the way and saw the dents and nicks at the slashing end of the blade.

You are not samurai.

The boy looked at him, trying to produce a scorn he did not feel, his tears overflowing now, sliding down both cheeks.

You carry weapons that are forbidden, and you have slain a man without justification. You are a crimi-nal.

Who are you to say it? cried the Hell-kite of Edo. He seized the front his robe with both hands and gripped it closed until his knuckles turned white. Who are you at all?

Who am I? I am someone who always arrives at where he is meant to be. Jirobei examined the neglected blade again then said, Sit up straighter.

You're not a person who can tell me what to do, the boy cried, his weeping eyes squeezing out frightened tears; but he did straighten his back in spite of himself, and his head came away without a moment of doubt, his life's blood leaping up from its neck stump in a sin-gle gasp then slowing and seeping out naturally.

Jirobei left the corpse where it sat while he went to gather dry wood. He built his pyre around the Hell-kite who still clutched the front of his robe in the obscene modesty of his fear, blood coating his hands and wrists and pooling in his lap. Jirobei piled his swords and the new-style gun there too, and added the two heads, one a disgrace, the other cut cleanly. He sat with the pyre even after it had burned down then moved farther off to choose his bivouac for that night.

Jirobei raked through the ashes at dawn and dragged out the blackened sword blades and the gun barrel with its lock and breech and firing mechanism charred. He broke the sword blades on the outcropping of granite. He used a loose rock to smash the breech with its flange cover and serpentine, but the gun barrel itself was too stiff to bend or break so he tossed it into a brushy gorge as a thing unworthy of respect.

The Plum Rains

梅 雨

She came back alone after first prayers and slid open her white paper doors. Misty drizzle filled the dense cedar forest surrounding the nunnery. The inside walls of her room were tacky with the damp, the tatami mats slick with it, and a faint grey dusting furred the brocade mat-bindings. It was a tired season, a time of melancholy wistfulness.

She had prayed that morning as she did every morning for the souls of those she had betrayed. The rain shutters of the Image Hall had been fastened in place, and the rows of kneeling women murmuring the wondrous words of the Lotus Sutra to the gentle thrumming of rain on the roofs and verandas were like a manifestation of the weight of the moisture in the air. It was the season for listlessness and regret, for longing for what could never be recovered.

But the faces of her dead no longer came to her. Nor did her terror flood up at their fear. Nor her remorse.

The nunnery for condemned women was located at the top end of a steep valley. A dry stream of raked pebbles separated Aoi's veranda corridor from the pressure of the trees on the hillside. It flowed past upright rocks configured like miniature islands and emptied finally into the absolving sea of raked gravel in the back garden. Most of the pebbles were the size of soy bean kernels – granite, ovoid, rolled smooth by centuries of tumbling in mountain cataracts – but some were as large as quail eggs; and she had brought one inside soon after her arrival and kept it for solace, for the sense of the small dry stone in the palm of her hand, of its being there as a specific weight and shape and texture that would never vary, never depart from the fact of itself. The pebble had possessed her as she possessed it; and although the nun Aoi had long since admitted to herself the foolishness of such thoughts, the pebble still had its place on her personal Buddha-shelf beside a small sandalwood statue of the Kannon Bodhisattva and the death plaques of the Hori family, the incised gold words faded now, the once glossy black lacquer surface now matte, and with hardly any scent remaining.

Aoi had joined her voice to the voices of the other condemned women, all of them bound together under the benevolent gaze of the Jizō Bodhisattva, guardian of children and wayfarers; and when Aoi prayed for the Hori, she made no distinction between the eldest son, who had died for love of her, and his parents and younger brothers, who had died as a result of his death. All of them would be waiting for her like wavering shadows on the yellow sands of hell, and she would hear their cries of torment and vituperation, for their lives had been denied them and the fault was hers.

Even throwing out wilted flowers is burdensome: the endless plum rains.

ONE OF THE NOVICES WAS standing in her doorway. She was a weepy little creature who smelled faintly of urine and still hoped for a different life even though the shogunate would never allow it for the simple reason that if one woman who had been sequestered unfairly were to be released then all those unfairly sequestered would begin clamouring for it. Punishing the innocent, Aoi knew, was more effective than punishing the guilty.

The abbess has requested your presence, said the little novice.

Now?

If it is acceptable…

Aoi was called in to receive devotional instructions occasionally although these interviews soon evolved into friendly chats. The abbess was also from a branch of the Imperial Family, and her concerns with sanctity were perfunctory. She had never been permitted to leave the compound, but she had seen men at a distance and understood in a vague way that they were in possession of distinctive if improbable anatomical characteristics so that Aoi had been obliged on occasion to share her previous experiences, describing in hushed tones events that had occurred in her presence, her own participation in them, what they had meant and why they had meant it. The older woman would ponder her description of these dubious encounters like someone hearing reports of a remote land where the sun shines at midnight and fires burn inside ice.

Aoi had scarcely seated herself when she was told she had visitors. An official from the shogunate was waiting to see her, and he was accompanied by a popular writer whose name was known to all who loved tales and stories.

Aoi reminded the abbess that she was not permitted to see others, but the woman only looked at her as if she were a fairy-phantom whose true incarnation had finally been revealed. The summons could not be ignored.

Aoi took one of the nunnery's yellow oil-paper umbrellas. The day was too humid for a cloak so she draped a white gauze shawl over her bald head like a loose hood and wore high clogs against the probability of the forecourt being muddy.

The mopey little novice trailed after her. She asked where she was going then before Aoi replied, asked if she could go with her.

The tedium of the fifth month rains: moss blooming on the old tombs also feels it.

AFTER HER HAIR HAD BEEN hacked off and her head shaved, she was left kneeling on the dirt of an enclosed courtyard-garden, her hands tied behind her back with her wrists lashed to her ankles. The weird lightness of the sense of the air on her naked scalp had astonished her. What a thing it was to feel the absence of your life's hair and accept that you were no longer any part of what you had been. She felt where the razor had nicked her. There was a constellation of blood drops on the thin layer of white silk stretched over her thighs, and she assumed there would be blood stains on the back of her robe too. She also assumed she was waiting to be killed.

The ropes binding her were too tight and her hands had gone numb. She wasn't afraid of dying although she was afraid of the pain of it. She tried touching her thumbs to her fingertips but felt nothing. And of the terror she would feel as her death began to happen.

An ant passed before her and she watched it out of sight, studying its asynchronous articulation. Her eyelids were crusted with dried tears, and gnats alighted there, drawn by the salty residue. She shook them away but they came back so she stopped doing it. There were other, smaller insects on the dirt, each walking in its own manner and following its own purpose; and she began singing softly to herself the toddler's song that she had been taught by a woman whose face she could no longer recall although every word of the silly little ditty came back to her. She thought she could remember the brief flickering of pleasure that she had brought to the sequestered palace women in their lonely chambers as she marched around on her fat little pink legs fearlessly singing in her baby's voice about the wind in the trees and the deer in the hills.

Except she wasn't remembering it, she was recalling having been told it. Her nurse's face, too, was not a memory but only a configuration of words that she had always accepted, as if the shape of the actual woman's face was nothing more substantial than mist burning off a meadow by the sun. How ungrateful she felt. Yet it was also certain that this was all she would ever have so she had better discover how to cherish it. My nurse loved me, she said, voicing it aloud the way a person might toss a stone into a deep pool to see if its bottom could be detected. But, still, all she knew about herself was what she'd been told. Her whole life had been made up of stories heard and remembered and repeated.

And wasn't what she had now, the phrases she was telling herself about herself, also self-assembled? The orphan's need for a narrative? The unwanted girl's hunger for memories? Yet other than these configurations, she had nothing.

And it seemed … paltry. But was it?

An ant like the one she'd seen before passed her knees, also wonderful in the method of its ambulation, its path like that of the other except following a slightly different trajectory. Had they begun at the same place? Would they end up together? Aoi knelt with her head down and felt the warmth of the sun on her naked skull and the tiny caresses of gnats in her eyelashes.

The decision to conclude matters was made late in the afternoon. The white paper doors were removed, and Aoi was confronted by a chamber opened like a pavilion and occupied by representatives of the shogunate. A personage too eminent to be identified sat on a dais behind a screen-of-state in the back half of the chamber. He would not demean himself by addressing her directly but spoke in a quiet voice to his steward, who listened with his head bowed then transferred his words.

It is instructed that you be told what will happen to you. Your adulterous lover has been chastised. But his family has asked to be allowed to atone for his crimes themselves. This family has always been a loyal vassal of the Tokugawa. It is wished therefore that some comfort be found for them.

Old Hori was brought into the courtyard with his wife and his two remaining sons. They were dressed in short white robes. Hori was calm although his wife, a plump woman with her hair configured in a provincial style, had been weeping; and the two young boys seemed frightened. None of them so much as glanced at Aoi. The handles of Hori's short sword and stabbing dagger had been replaced with simple ones of paulownia wood, and the naked blades were wrapped in pure white paper. Hori's assistant, a young warrior from his domain, came in behind him, his long sword carried still sheathed.

The Hori family knelt in front of the veranda where the steward sat. They bowed together, the younger boy mistiming it by starting too late and ending too soon.

Guards brought out the head of her lover, Hori Ushimaru, affixed to a viewing stand. They placed it like a watcher on the edge of the veranda, and the younger boy cried out but his mother silenced him.

Old Hori stated his name and his lineage. He declared that the Hori family had always supported the Tokugawa Shogunate and would always continue to do so. He acknowledged he was at fault for allowing his son to misbehave with an orphan of the palace, and he accepted that this was unforgivable. He agreed to atone for it. His wife would accompany him. But he wished to request humbly that his remaining sons be spared. Their lives had only just begun. More should be allotted to them. Old Hori bowed again, touching his forehead to the dirt of the courtyard and held it there.

The steward had listened to this plea with displeasure. Would your sons not remember your death? And wish to avenge you? How would your loyalty to the Tokugawa appear then? And if they attempted revenge and found success, then their actions would create more disharmony. And if they failed, then the shame of that would be an added burden to them. And how much worse would that burden be if they were unable even to make an attempt?

No, Hori, your boys do not merit such an uncertain fate. The natural flow of things is the better one.

The kneeling samurai lifted his head and observed the steward then bowed again in submission. He took up his short sword. He removed the purification paper then touched the blade reverently to his brow. His middle son knelt upright with his back very straight. For the life you have given me, I thank you. His knees were spread apart and his ankles crossed properly so that he would not topple over sideways. And for preceding you, I apologise. He waited with his head up, his hands on the tops of his thighs, and his eyes fixed on the steward. His father took him across the throat quickly and deeply, and the suddenness of the blood-release came as a part of his folding forward at the shock of it.

His father held him until he stopped quivering then rolled him onto his back and straightened his garments.

The younger boy had to be soothed by his mother. He buried his face in her bosom. She shielded him and calmed him then shifted him around, still holding him in her arms but presenting his throat. The younger boy's blood soaked into the front of his mother's death robe as she drew him back into her embrace and cradled him as he died then released him and allowed his father to place him beside his brother.

Hori's wife had worn two inner sashes, as befits a samurai's wife, and she removed the extra one now and bound her legs together across the thighs so that her skirt would not open indecorously. Her husband removed the purification paper from the short stabbing dagger then touched the naked blade to his forehead in acknowledgement. He bowed to her. She returned his bow, both her palms pressing down on the hard earth that her forehead also touched. She straightened herself and regarded him. Well, then, if it must be so, she said, and took the short knife in both hands. She held it reversed in front of her breast so that the blade was pointing upward. She was not a strong woman, but what strength she had would now be the gift she could extend, and she threw herself forward, diving onto the blade, driving the point of it up under her jaw for the death she would find there.

Her thrust cut off-centre, and she lay shuddering on her side, the knife embedded under her jaw and her blood draining out over it but no easy death arriving. One hand had been knocked off the hilt and it grabbed at the dirt of the courtyard, scraping at it as if digging there, forming ridges the way the receding tide leaves wave-patterns in the sand, then doing that less and less then no longer doing it.

Old Hori smoothed down the hem of her robe. He let his hand rest for a moment on her ankle. Then he sat back and stripped off the top of his death robe by lifting his arms out. He tucked the sleeves under his feet to help keep his body aligned. His assistant came up behind him with his sword unsheathed. Hori wrapped a thick white hand cloth around the blade of his small sword so that he could grip it below the hilt. He instructed his assistant to permit him to finish the entire ritual. I thank the shogunate for this opportunity to redeem my son and myself, Hori said. He sat for a moment very still. Then he inhaled and with a shout stabbed the blade into the side of his abdomen, gasping like someone plunged in cold water. Using both hands he dragged the blade across slicing deeply so that in the spill of blood slobber the first blue loops of intestines slithered out squirming onto his thighs. His face drained to white and his eyes locked. He pulled out the blade and stabbed it inwards a second time, jerking it upwards with his head pressed forward straining against the shriek of it and his attendant hit him perfectly so that his head landed between his knees and his corpse remained kneeling upright, blood draining out of his neck-stump, both hands still gripping the blade locked in his belly.

The steward leaned back to listen to the man behind the screen then turned to Aoi again. He stared at her for a long moment then signalled for her ropes to be cut. Aoi was pulled to her feet and held upright by her guards, her legs too weak to support her.

You are not to be given a Buddhist name. You have no family name. You will continue to be called Aoi, but this word will be written with kana syllables only. You will stay all your life where we put you. No other activity will be allowed, no travel, no visits, no walks in the hills. You are only a thing waiting to die.

The august personage spoke again and the steward listened bowing then straightened up and said, If you violate any of these arrangements, you will be burned in a fire and twenty others living nearby will be chosen at random and burned in it with you. Men, women, children will be selected to die because of you, and their deaths will also burden your soul. Is there any part of this you don't understand?

Aoi said nothing at first then lifted her head slightly with her eyes still on the earth before her and said, I understand it.

You will travel tomorrow on your last road. You will take the Hori funerary plaques with you. And each morning and each evening you will offer prayers for the repose of the souls of the Hori. That is what you will do. And it is all you will ever do.

An evening shower, on the veranda railing hang forgotten robes of silk gauze.

THE SHOGUNATE OFFICIAL STOOD waiting alone beside the trunk of an immense cedar that was girded by a sanctity rope, the sodden white paper streamers of which hung limply in the endless drizzle. Ox-Blossom told her he had been sent as an emissary of the Tokugawa family. He said changes had occurred which would affect her. He told her a writer from Edo had also come with him. Chibi-kun is widely admired for his florid imagination, said Ox-blossom. He will join us once you and I have reached an agreement.

Chibi-kun?

His stories are popular in the pleasure quarters, and his librettos for the theatre are admired.

When Aoi seemed to have nothing to say to this, Ox-blossom explained that the new shogun had begun reviewing many of the policies established by his predecessor. It has been decided to rehabilitate the Hori Clan. Their death plaques would be moved to the family's mortuary temple. Ox-Blossom bowed his head in polite recognition that this news might come as a surprise to her, rain-flow sliding off the front brim of his round hat. He straightened up and said, Your own name will also be returned to you.

Aoi began strolling around the edge of the forecourt, following a path that led up towards the nunnery's cemetery, and Ox-blossom followed after her. A stream flowed beside the path, and the far bank was lined with irises, the deep indigo petals beaded with rain.

I decline it, Aoi said. I've been buried here.

She stood beside a carved granite hand-washing basin that stood at the back corner of the outer hall. A file of flat black stones had been positioned under where runoff from the eaves would drip.

I have no wish for a name to survive me.

Probably I have expressed myself poorly, Ox-Blossom said. By granting you your name, the shogun is also restoring your access to the world...

Aoi did not respond, but her head tilted forward slightly under the amber rain-light of her umbrella, and the shadows on her face darkened so that the official hesitated then said, You can go where you wish. Do what you choose. Young Chibi-kun has ideas. He wants to write the story of your life. He feels there is money to be made.

Aoi stared at him. My life…?

Chibi-kun is clever with words.

Aoi said nothing. But as she looked at the shogun's official, her face softened with sadness at memories of the past; and unsure as to whether or not she seemed about to reconsider her refusal, the shogunate emissary tried to encourage her, saying that she would be surprised by the changes in the world, for nothing she had known was as it had been.

The rains of the fifth month: and within what has been lost, what remains.

Notes on Poems and Translations

All poems are by Matsuo Bashō unless otherwise indicated; all translations are my own. Poems in the stories not listed here are pastiches of my own devising, based on Japanese or Chinese models.

Page 7 – 'A summer downpour in the mountains, and the wild monkeys also seem to want little rain capes.' Bashō is working out the idea that becomes the famous 'First winter showers: the monkeys also seem to want rice-straw rain coats.' *Hatsushigure / saru mo komino o / hoshigenari.* This poem also supplies the title to *Saru-mino*, Bashō most prized collection (in English translation: *The Monkey's Straw Raincoat*).

Page 13 – 'Morning dew on the damp earth, and the muddy melons seem cool.' *Asatsuyu ni / yogorete suzushi / uri no tsuchi.* (Summer 1694)

Page 30 – 'Under the same roof, pleasure providers also are sleeping: bushclover and the moon.' *Hitotsu ya ni / yūjo mo netari / hagi to tsuki.* (Autumn 1689)

Page 33 – Both Ohasu's haiku are actually by Enomoto Kikaku (1661–1707), one of Bashō's followers. *Yūdachi ya / ie wo megurite / naku ahiru* and *Yūdachi ya / hitori soto miru / onna kana.*

Page 36 – Ohasu's quote is a reference to a waka by early Heian female poet Ono no Komachi (fl. ca. 850): *Hito ni awan / tsuki no naka ni wa / omoiokite / mune hashiribi ni / kokoro yakeori.*

Page 37 – 'The white poppy: wings torn off a butterfly as a keepsake.' *Shirageshi ni / hane mogu chō no / katami kana.* (Summer 1685)

Page 69 – 'Without merit but also without guilt: winter seclusion.' *Nō nashi wa / tsumi mo mata nashi / fuyugomori.* Kobayashi Issa (1763–1827)

Page 100 – 'The first snowfall, what happiness to be in my own house.' *Hatsuyuki ya / saiwai an ni / makariaru.* (Winter 1686)

Page 102 – 'On an old gilt screen, the image of an ancient pine: winter seclusion.' *Kinbyō no / matsu no furusa yo / fuyugomori.* (Winter 1694)

Page 109 – 'The charcoal banked; but on the wall, the guest's shadow.' *Uzumibi ya / kabe ni wa kyaku no / kage-bōshi.* (Winter 1693)

Page 129 'Clouds of cherry blossoms: is the temple bell at Ueno? at Akasaka?' *Hana no kumo / kane wa ueno ka / akasaka ka.* (Spring 1687)

Page 131 – 'Spring arrives in the faint haze that wreathes these nameless hills.' *Haru nare ya / na mo nake yama no / usugasumi.* (Spring 1685)

Page 133 – 'Recollecting various things: the blooming of cherry blossoms.' *Samazama no / koto omoidasu / sakura kana.* (Spring 1688)

Page 134 – 'Under the trees, soup and fish salad too: cherry blossoms.' *Ki no moto ni / shiru mo namasu mo / sakura kana.* (Spring 1690)

Page 137 – 'Bats too come out into this floating world of birds and flowers.' *Kōmori mo / ideyo ukiyo no / hana ni tori.* (Spring 1685)

Page 139 – 'The sound of the bell fades, but the scent of blossoms continues: an evening.' *Kane kiete / hana no ka wa tsuku / yūbe kana.* (Spring 1684)

Page 143 – 'Only briefly above the blossoming trees: tonight's moon.' *Shibaraku wa / hana no ue naru / tsukiyo kana.* (Spring 1691)

Page 144 & page 203 – 'Ill while traveling, in my dreams still wandering over withered fields.' *Tabi ni yande / yume wa kareno wo / kakemeguru.* (Winter, 1694, Bashō's last poem)

Page 186 – 'On leafless branches, crows are settling: autumn twilight' *Kare eda ni / karasu no tomarikeri / aki no kure.* (Autumn 1680)

Page 190 – 'Speaking of things chills the lips: the autumn wind.' *Mono ieba / kuchibiru samushi / aki no kaze.* (Autumn 1684)

Page 194 – 'Along this road goes no one: autumn twilight.' *Kono michi ya / yuku hito nashi ni / aki no kure.* (Autumn 1694)